D1572252

# THEY HIDE

## SHORT STORIES TO TELL IN THE DARK

# THEY HIDE

## SHORT STORIES TO TELL IN THE DARK

## By Francesca Maria

Edited by Elle Turpitt
Proofread and formatted by Stephanie Ellis

Cover illustration and design by Kealan Patrick Burke

First Edition: April 2023

ISBN (paperback): 9781957537481
ISBN (ebook): 9781957537474
Library of Congress Control Number: 2023932804

BRIGIDS GATE PRESS
Bucyrus, Kansas
www.brigidsgatepress.com

Printed in the United States of America

*For Teresa and Angela, for sharing their love of King, Rice, Barker and all things that go bump in the night.*

Content warnings are provided at the end of the book

# CONTENTS

# PREFACE

Monsters have always fascinated me; the shadowy figures that hide in our nightmares and come out when we are at our weakest. Where do they come from, and do they exist without victims to prey upon? Are the dark things part of our collective imagination, or a deep-rooted evil we refuse to see within ourselves? Or, as I've struggled to understand my entire adult life: Are they real?

I grew up in a haunted house. We were plagued by a constant presence that refused to give us any privacy or peace. Lights flickered, TVs would go on and off, footsteps were heard across the empty attic. Dolls would open their eyes, and something scratched from the inside of our closets as if trying to escape. My siblings and I have different memories of that house on the hill, and as adults we try to rationalize what we lived through.

At the age of six I wrote my first horror story, a reflection of my own experiences at the time. It was about a group of kids who went into a haunted house at the end of a dreary lane. It was pretty impressive for a six-year-old; I remember it being over ten pages long. I wish I still had it, but it has been lost to time. I have been writing horror ever since. Every time I pen a story, I'm looking for answers, for some insight or clue into what I experienced in my youth. And to this day, I am still searching.

The collection you have before you is my exploration into horror's most beloved monsters: witches, vampires, demons, ghosts, mummies, aliens and the like. My library is filled with anthologies dedicated to each of these classic icons, and I love reading various writers' interpretations of these well-worn characters. I wanted to take my crack at it and write versions of my own. The work you have in front of you is my love letter to the nightmares that haunt my waking world. Enjoy.

# THE WYSTERFIELD MURDERS

When Goody Sarah went to fetch the daily water, she noticed her friend Goody Margaret was not there. Sarah and Margaret would meet at the well each morning and discuss their plans for the day. Margaret's friendship was one of a few comforts Sarah experienced in the town of Wysterfield. Today, her friend was nowhere to be found and Sarah was alone.

Margaret was also absent at the church for devotion that morning.

While Sarah pondered her friend's absence, she noticed something reflective shining up at her from the bottom of the well. Was it a stone? No, it was too deep for any sun to cast a light. A piece of metal reflecting off the water? Metal was so scarce, no one would be so careless as to lose it in the well. Goody Sarah squinted with her hawk eyes, but the object eluded her.

The prayer bells chimed, and Goody Sarah abandoned her task and heeded the call to church. The bell, like the church itself, was small but impressive—being one of the few objects that had traveled from the Old World. The bell had been hoisted up the steeple of the church by the esteemed Reverend William Glenhock Sr. nearly ten years ago. The whole town came to witness its placement. It was a proud day for Wysterfield.

The bell rang twice a day, once for morning devotion and once for evening prayer before the communal supper. So when the church bell rang mid-morning, Sarah knew something was amiss. The bell never rang outside of prayer time.

Walking up to the churchyard, Sarah observed Goody Rebecca and her son Nathan as they scurried into the church. Sarah caught

3

Rebecca's eye and recognized a look of fear. As she entered the church, Sarah noticed that nearly all of the townsfolk were in attendance. Within a few more minutes, the pews were full. All were present, or so it seemed.

The distinguished Reverend William Glenhock Jr. approached the pulpit, looking grave with less than his usual ferocity.

"Dear, good folk of Wysterfield," he began. "It pains me to tell you that Goodman Richard Garrett, his wife Goody Margaret, and their children, were found slain in their home this morning. Deacon Josiah discovered the bodies when he went to inquire as to why they had missed morning devotion."

"Oh no!" Sarah shrieked, barely audible against the cries that had erupted from the congregation. Panicked questions rose up through the noise.

"Who did this?"

"How could this have happened?"

"Was it the natives?"

"We'll all be murdered in our sleep!"

Fear quickly consumed the humble crowd.

"Calm yourselves please, calm yourselves," assured Rev. Glenhock. "Remember, God is on our side. We are protected by His Grace. This was clearly an act of the Devil himself! And the Fallen Angel cannot gain entry into your soul unless you invite him in!"

Seeing the wheels turn in the heads of his congregation, Rev. Glenhock seized the moment. "Goodman Richard and his family *must* have been in league with the Devil! They were deceived by his trickery, let their guard down and allowed evil into their home. For there is no question, my fair people, the Devil has come to Wysterfield!"

A leaden silence fell upon the crowd as they processed what the good reverend proclaimed. Eyes darted at each other from lowered heads.

Goody Sarah, devastated by the news of her friend, was not as easily swayed by Glenhock's words as some of her fellow townspeople. She had come to the New World to seek freedom and tolerance. She was a woman of great faith who feared no man and this, Sarah felt, was the work of man.

And she refused to believe, as Reverend Glenhock put it, that the Devil would have found a way into Goody Margaret's soul. *Impossible*, thought Goody Sarah. Though, she admitted to herself, she didn't know Goodman Richard all that well. She tended to keep away from the men. Sarah never did quite trust them.

As the congregation found their legs again, a small group of elders joined Reverend Glenhock at the front of the church. They chatted in hushed whispers about what to do with the bodies, along with the Garretts' property and possessions.

Goody Sarah looked on as the church emptied. She felt an ache in her heart as she thought of Goody Margaret and her twin boys, Jonathan and James. Goody Margaret once nursed Sarah back to health after she nearly died of the same fever that took her own dear husband, Robert, five years before. It was a kindness Sarah never forgot.

It was decided among the women to prepare the bodies for burial and the men would build the caskets. The Garrett family's remains must be interred into the good earth of the Lord before sunset if their souls were to be saved from the clutches of eternal damnation.

Goody Sarah walked, stunned, back to her cottage at the edge of town. Her head was pounding, and she heard her heartbeat inside her ears. This was not right. What could have done this to an entire family?

How could no one have heard a cry for help? Goody Clara and her husband Matthew were just yards away from the Garrett home. Heat rushed up her spine as her adrenaline replayed what Goody Margaret must have felt.

The sun beat down on her as it approached midday. She gathered her pail, brushes, and lye soap, and found some old rags towards the back of the cupboard. As her head continued to pound, she knelt at the side of her bed and prayed.

\*\*\*

Outside the churchyard, the men brought together all the spare lumber to see what they had and what they would still need. There was a partially built structure near the creek which had been left abandoned when the cold winter months set in. Whatever additional lumber they would need could be harvested there.

Within a few hours, four coffins were nearly completed, sanded down and smoothed from the inside out.

\*\*\*

When Goody Sarah arrived at the Garrett home, she felt her head throb once again and a feeling of nausea swept through her body. She was not the first to arrive. Goody Mary was rinsing out sheets in front of the house. Goody Mary was made of stern stock. The oldest of the women, she had survived her husband, Goodman Simon, going on eight years now. Goody Mary was the first to teach Sarah how to plow her own fields and harvest her crops when Robert died. She would also take Sarah out hunting, showing her how to properly trap, kill, and skin rabbits—and even deer. So when Goody Sarah saw a look of terror in Goody Mary's eyes, she knew what she was walking into must be horrific.

The smell hit her first, like a full outhouse exposed to the afternoon sun, mixed with rotting meat. Next came the sound, a low and constant thrumming. Sarah's eyes identified black flurries moving in clusters. Flies. The Garrett's home was alive with swarms of black flies, buzzing in a violent fervor.

Sarah's gaze followed the moving black cloud over a motionless shape in the two-room cabin. Goodman Richard was slumped at the kitchen table with one arm stretched over his head, as if his shirt were being pulled off. He sat stiff in the kitchen chair, the contents of his bowels dried up on the floor beneath him. His upper torso lay sideways on the table, one hand under his head as if in slumber, the other pulled unnaturally over his ear and head so his hand stretched the length of the table. Then Sarah saw his eyes. His eyes were three times their normal size—almost as if something behind his sockets had kicked them out beyond their lids. So horrified was Sarah, she had to step out to the landing again with Goody Mary to keep from screaming.

"What happened in there is the Devil's work," Goody Mary said in a cry that came like a shout.

Sarah, still stunned, only nodded. She had seen death before. When her Robert died, the fever took months to ravage his body. It started with the yellowish skin, then each of his appendages swelled to the point of bursting. By the time he finally died, Sarah felt relief that his suffering was at an end. He was barely recognizable before the Lord took him, except for his eyes. She could still find glimpses of him through his eyes.

Sarah took another long deep breath of fresh air, and went back inside the cabin. She walked past the contorted body of Goodman Richard and into the sleeping quarters. Jonathan and James were huddled together in each other's arms, still in their dressing gowns. Sarah scanned their bodies. They looked almost peaceful, nothing seemed amiss—until she saw their faces. Two heads locked together, forehead to forehead, nose to nose, with huge bulging eyes. There was something unnatural about their appearance; their faces were the wrong shape, much like their father's. But it was their enlarged eyes, fixed on each other's with a look of frozen terror that drew Sarah's focus.

Goody Sarah pulled the bed curtain back further and jumped at the sight of Goody Margaret holding her boys. How Sarah had missed her was a mystery. Encircling the twins were Margaret's stockinged legs, her feet stiff in her brown boots. The boys were nestled together between their mother's opened legs, almost as if they were newly born. Above the boys' heads, their mother sat, slouched forward with her head lolled to one side. She had on her nightgown and bonnet, her work skirt was affixed to her waist.

Margaret's mouth was open—revealing a tongue that dangled too long down the side of her face. Her eyes, like the rest of the family's, had bulged out of their sockets, though hers were freed completely from their compartment and were hanging precariously upon her cheeks.

Goody Sarah heard a piercing sound far off in the distance. She realized it was her own screaming. Sarah turned and ran from the cottage once again.

Out on the landing, Sarah scarcely observed the rest of the women arriving. One by one they discovered the horror, screaming and crying as their senses were assaulted on all fronts. Some were unable to hold down their breakfast and the sound of retching made Sarah reflexively dry heave. After what seemed like too long and no time at all, the women were out in front of the house, shocked, horrified and unable to process what they had witnessed. It was then that the worshipful Reverend Glenhock made his presence known.

"Good women, you have seen firsthand the work of Lucifer, alive and well in our little town. Take heed lest you be next on his list!" spat the reverend.

Few of the women were aware enough of their surroundings to hear Glenhock's voice. Some nodded, acknowledging that words had been spoken.

"Come, we must make haste. Their bodies may be lost but their souls may still be embraced by the great Almighty above!"

Slowly the women, led by Goody Mary, returned to the cottage and began the grim task of cleaning and preparing the bodies for burial.

Goody Sarah took it upon herself to prepare Goody Margaret, her friend. As the boys were removed from the bed, Sarah reached in and grabbed Goody Margaret's hands. They were cold and stiff to the touch. Hanging onto her boys for dear life, Sarah imagined. She tried to pull Margaret's body forward, closer to the edge of the bed, but she seemed stuck. She tugged a few more times until she heard a wet suction noise and realized Goody Margaret had soiled herself, the contents cementing her squarely to the bed. With more force, Sarah freed Margaret, but the weight knocked her off balance and Sarah found herself falling backwards onto the hard floor. As if in slow motion, Goody Margaret's body fell on top of Sarah. She was pinned to the floor by the deadweight of her friend. Margaret's blonde hair crept out from under her bonnet and gently kissed Sarah's cheek.

Sarah felt something wet with a cold stickiness land on her shoulder. Goody Margaret's long, lolling tongue had found its way out of its perch and onto Goody Sarah's collarbone. Sarah was reminded of the earthworms she used to pluck out of the garden when she was a child. Sarah heard footsteps as help arrived, and she was released from Goody Margaret's embrace.

The menfolk had entered the cottage, taking measurements for the coffins before the last panels were placed. At this point, all able-bodied townsfolk were helping to prepare the burial. Children were kept at a distance at Goody Ester's home. The murmurs and shrieks continued as the gravity of the murders fell onto each of the townspeople.

*"This was no animal, there were no bites taken out of the bodies."*

*"This was unnatural, there was not a drop of blood!"*

*"This was not the work of the Perquots."*

***

Before the supper bell rang, four bodies, cleaned and dressed, had been laid out on the makeshift platform in front of the home. Sweat, tears, and muck were caked onto the townspeople as they placed the corpses into their respective coffins. Goodman Zachariah and Goodman Elizar had to forcibly manipulate Goodman Richard and Goody Margaret to get them to lie flat in their coffins as the stiffness of death had already set upon them.

The reverend went about his task with the exuberance of one who felt he had the upper hand. He instructed the townspeople to bring the coffins to the church where he would say the final blessing. The town watched as the lids of the coffins were nailed shut, closing out the sun for all eternity. A few used the washbasin outside the church to cleanse their face and hands before entering God's holy place. Goody Sarah was one of the last to enter. Still in shock, still unable to process what she'd seen and the task she'd performed. She took a seat towards the back next to Goody Mary.

"Good people of Wysterfield. You have done God's work today, and for that you will be rewarded in the eyes of the Lord, for there is no greater love than the love you show to your neighbor. The Garrett family, though corrupted by the snake on the tree of life himself, have sinned against God and sinned against His covenants. Why else would this tragedy have befallen them? For this was not the work of animals, no. And this was not the work of the Perquots with whom we've had peace these last eight years. No. No. Those of you who saw the evil that has beset this family know in your hearts that this was no act of man. The way their bodies were tortured, the pain of it—and yet, no cries were heard, no blood was spilled. No action was taken by Goodman Richard to defend his family. And why not, my good people? Because the Devil himself, the Fallen Angel of God, sent to tempt and torment the weak, slid under their door at the break of dawn and took their souls back to the pits of Hell. But remember, my fellow followers of Christ, that the Devil cannot gain entry unless *you let him in*!" And with that, Reverend Glenhock slammed the Bible down on the pulpit, knocking a candle over in the process. "Now we," he asserted, "as a community can come together in Jesus's name to ask for forgiveness and deliverance for their souls before Satan has branded them his. We have, until the sun sets, an opportunity to free them of their suffering by anointing their bodies with God's grace and benevolence. Join me brothers and sisters as we, together, anoint their caskets with the blessed oil of Christ himself, the Savior from whom all good things come."

One by one, members of the congregation walked up to the caskets and sprinkled the christened oil on all four wooden boxes. When it was Sarah's turn, she looked to Goody Mary for guidance but found only a blank stare. She stood, took her place and, as she sprinkled the oil, whispered, "God's grace be with you, my friend."

A tear fell, followed by another, until their constant stream formed lines down Sarah's face.

The reverend then instructed a dozen of the men to carry the coffins out into the churchyard. The holes were dug and ready to accept their new occupants. Carefully, with the plow harnesses, they lowered the coffins into their graves. When they got to the last casket, that of Goodman Richard, the strap strained and protested, then with no further warning, snapped, sending the large wooden box into the hole. One of the coffin slats broke, revealing the protruding eyes of its occupant. Several women screamed and one fainted, while the men rushed to right the entombment. An elder ran to the stack of wood used earlier to make the caskets and, with the help of a few more hands, quickly replaced the broken plank. Like the anointed oil, each of the townspeople tossed a shovel of dirt into the graves until the wood was no longer visible.

Sunset had fallen, and the exhausted, stunned people of Wysterfield retired to their homes, forgoing supper and settling instead for a restless night's sleep.

\*\*\*

Sarah dreamed that night. She dreamed of her friend Goody Margaret dancing in a field of wildflowers. The clouds turned dark and Margaret's limbs started to decay until she collapsed onto the grass which turned into black mush. The ground moved as hundreds of maggots consumed whatever morsel was left. In Sarah's dream, Margaret's face stared back at her with eyes that slowly bulged until finally, painfully, they dislodged themselves from their sockets.

Sarah awoke with a scream. Sweat poured down her back, plastering her hair to her face. She heard footsteps and hushed voices outside her cabin. She went to the window to see a few shapes hurrying off into the woods. The exhaustion of the day caught up with her. Just as she thought to go investigate, she collapsed back into her bed.

***

Three weeks passed with little or no investigation. Glenhock battled Satan at the pulpit, trying to exorcize any demons lingering from the Garrett family. A few of the elders went to talk with the Chief of the Perquots, but they had no desire to start a war with their trading partners. The Perquots saw more profit to be had by the townspeople. Trade was good.

Life slowly returned to normal in Wysterfield. This troubled Sarah, as she did not understand how her fellow brethren could so soon forget about the gruesome slayings of the Garretts. Did they really believe Rev. Glenhock's rhetoric about the Devil killing the family? Surely, even if Satan was involved, he would have needed a person to carry out the horrific deed—but whom? Who had the time or capacity to think through and carry out such a grisly task undetected?

Sarah thought of her fellow townsmen in a new light. Goodman Caleb and Goodman Elias were too old and frail to commit such a murder. She ruled out Goodman Josiah and Goodman Levi because they had been out on a hunting party the week of the murders. That still left over six dozen individuals who could have had a hand in the killings. She knew at least two healthy adults were involved, maybe more. Then she remembered the sounds she had heard in the woods the night following the Garrett murders. She felt the prickle of a thought at the back of her mind but could not quite reach it. As she felt it starting to materialize, a woman screamed in the distance.

Goody Sarah ran off towards the sound, following others who were already in pursuit. Goody Temperance was hovering near the river's edge, pointing at a white object floating near the washing shallows.

As Sarah approached to get a closer look, the shape of a woman appeared, with a bonnet still affixed. Goodman Matthew and Goodman Ezekiel raced into the water to retrieve the woman, who was now a few feet from shore. As they turned her over, a cacophony of screams filled the spring air. Goody Mary, with her white hair loose around her face, had eyes bulging outside of their sockets, and her tongue lay lifeless in an unhinged jaw.

Another close tie to Sarah had fallen victim to whatever was plaguing their town. Sarah ran to the body, touching it, then beating it, hoping for life to return. She was met with a gray stare as Goody Mary's body remained still and quiet. A fury of emotions erupted in Sarah until she could no longer hold it in, and she expelled the contents of her stomach into the stream.

As the men carried the body to the church, Sarah noticed something red beneath Goody Mary's undergarments. Was it a birthmark or a cut? Sarah struggled to identify it as the waterlogged skin had hidden its details.

Goody Mary had always been a bit outside of society. She was an independent thinker, not shy about speaking her mind to the elders of the town. When a discussion in the church courtyard broke out on whether to re-till the corn fields or start anew, Goody Mary was the first to express her opinion. When young Nathaniel fell off a high tree, Goody Mary was the one who mended his bones. She was a widow, and a mother to none, and seen as an equal to man—as much as a woman could be in the patriarchal village. Goody Mary was respected by both men and women alike. She spoke sense in a new land where level heads were needed.

So how could this have happened to her? Who or what was behind it? Sarah pulled herself up off the ground and waited for her head to stop spinning. She closed her eyes and found her feet beneath her. The church bell rang in earnest. It was a frantic call urging all to gather once again.

\*\*\*

Once inside the church, Sarah saw a figure pacing from one end of the altar to the other. It was Glenhock, in a fevered state that frightened her. When he spoke, she jumped, startled by his crazed, high-pitched volume.

"The Devil has come to collect another soul! Yes, yes, he has!"
he began. "For when you make a deal with the Devil, he comes to
collect! Mark my words, gentle townspeople, Goody Mary was a
bride of Satan himself!"

Gasps and cries were heard within the hall.

"No!"

"It cannot be!"

"Impossible!"

"Good Lord above, save us!"

Sensing the crowd's skepticism, Reverend Glenhock continued.
"You do not know which is good or evil by anything other than the
fruit of the tree. For Matthew 7:15 states, 'Beware of false
prophets who came to you in sheep's clothing, but inwardly they
are ravenous wolves! You will know them by their fruits. Every
good tree bears good fruit but a bad tree bears bad fruit. Every tree
that does not bear good fruit is cut down and thrown into the fire.
Therefore, by their fruits you will know them!' Now let me ask you
good people, what fruits did Goody Mary produce? Why did the
good Lord not grant her the fruit of a child, the holiest gift
bestowed onto women?

"I will tell you why! It is because the Lord found her unworthy!
Her womb was not sacred enough to hold the gift of life. She was
not good enough to house a soul. Yes, dear people, and you know
why. You know if you search deep enough into your hearts you will
know the answer."

Not a soul moved or breathed. Eyes avoided others' stares for
fear of the words about to be spoken.

The young reverend continued, "We all knew Goody Mary to
be a just and contributing member of our community. Goodman
Zachariah, she helped you when your crops turned before last
harvest. Goody Rachel, she helped mend your son's arm after he
fell out of that oak. I ask you, where did she get the knowledge to
do this? Her husband's been long dead these past eight years. She
did not read and was not schooled. So, I ask you, where did all that
knowledge come from? The Devil has all manner of knowledge."

Glenhock turned and whispered something to Deacon Josiah, who turned and went out the back door of the church.

In less than a minute, Deacon Josiah burst through the front doors of the church, pushing a wheelbarrow with the body of Goody Mary lying face up and half-naked for all to see. The pews were alive with gasps and screams. Women covered their children's eyes as they themselves looked away.

Once Deacon Josiah reached the altar, Rev. Glenhock reveled in the reaction of his congregation. He walked up to Mary's body and ripped open her undershirt. Full screams filled the church walls. "For this, good Christians," concluded the reverend, "is the mark of Satan himself! Found over Goody Mary's heart."

Sarah could now see the mark that had eluded her earlier. It was an inverted cross, cut with precision, stretching from Mary's collarbone down to her navel.

Glenhock continued, "Goody Mary pledged herself to Satan and became his bride! And today, good people, today he came to collect what is his!"

Pandemonium broke out as everyone rushed to exit the church, as if being in the presence of the Devil's concubine would somehow infect them with the same evil. Most everyone left, save Goody Sarah. Sarah, in the throes of grief for her friend, went from shock to anger. Her friend would not have fallen victim to temptation. Mary was a good, holy woman—but how did that mark come upon her chest?

Reverend Glenhock was wide-eyed with fervor. He'd uncovered the devil in their midst, and a look of pride and conviction poured over his countenance. In seeing Goody Sarah still in her pew, he advanced towards her in earnest.

"Why, Goody Sarah, are you in shock for seeing the Devil's wife? Do you seek council, given the fragility of your nature?"

With that last sentence, Sarah's eyes moved from her friend's bare-chested corpse and looked firmly into the eyes of Glenhock.

"You mistake my stillness for shock, Reverend, for I am in full control of my faculties. I am observing the poor mistreatment of a good woman, a woman who has done nothing but help this community." Her reply was even, steady.

Glenhock retorted, "Do you not see the mark about her chest? Do you deny it?"

"No …" Sarah hesitated, "I do not know how it got there."

*But I intend to find out*, she thought to herself. Sarah stood, approached Mary's body, and covered her friend's chest with her own handkerchief. Then she turned and left the church.

\*\*\*

The town was in a complete panic. Children were running wild and unattended. Crops were not being tilled, and household chores were abandoned. Everyone was traveling from house to house, whispering and gossiping about what they had witnessed.

*"I always knew there was something odd about that old woman, the way her crops grew when all others failed,"* said one.

*"I never understood why she did not keep a husband once her first one died. It is not natural to live without a husband, to have no children,"* said another.

Sarah caught wind of these murmurs as she made her way back to her cottage. Her blood was filled with rage, making the back of her neck hot. Now two of her confidantes were dead and both accused of dancing with the Devil. *Stuff and nonsense*, Sarah thought. *Complete and utter nonsense!*

\*\*\*

That night Sarah's dreams were wild once again. This time, Goody Mary and Goody Margaret were walking in a meadow, arm-in-arm, their backs to Sarah. They were humming *In the Light of the Valley*, and were laughing and carrying on. Sarah called out to them but they did not answer. She reached out a hand. Before she could touch one of their shoulders, they both turned and hissed at her— their long tongues dangling onto their housecoats. As she stared at them in horror, they mouthed in unison: *"Why donnnnnnnnsssssst youuuuuuu joinnnnnnnssssssss ussssss?"*

Again Sarah woke with a start, her heart pounding, her head racing. Grief and fear overtook her. What happened to her friends?

She put on her shift and stepped out into the night air to catch her breath. She knew it was just a dream, but it shook her to her core. A coyote cried in the distance and Sarah closed herself in, leaving the night to fend for itself.

*** 

The next morning, Sarah woke renewed and determined. She packed what she needed for her journey, shut up her windows, and placed a makeshift lock over her door as she set out west, towards the Perquots and hopefully to find answers. She left a short note for Goody Lydia asking her to keep an eye on her garden, and saying she would return in a few days after gathering seed for the next planting season.

She mounted her gray-spotted Appaloosa, Jacob, and within minutes was deep in the wilderness, the village left buried by trees and thicket. Jacob was a good workhorse. He had helped till her fields for over a decade. He was a sturdy companion and made Sarah feel comforted on the desolate trail.

The Perquots' settlement was a day's journey along the river. She made good time by dusk, and found a clearing surrounded by steep granite rocks, providing a safe enclosure for her to bed down for the night. She quickly built a fire with the kindling and flint she'd brought with her.

Being alone in the wilderness did not frighten Sarah. She knew what was out there: coyotes, wolves, deer, mountain lions and even bears—all of which kept clear of the fire. And with her keen ear, she'd hear them coming long before they got anywhere near her camp. She felt oddly peaceful; the first peace since before the murders. Man, she feared, but not nature. Nature had rules, guidelines. If one knows the rules, things are safe, predictable.

What happed to the Garrett family, to Goody Mary, was not natural. There was no order or reason for it. It was unpredictable. That scared Sarah more than anything else. As she drifted off to sleep, Sarah was haunted by the tortured faces of her friends.

Her dreams, fueled by the night air, became vivid and wild. A creature, covered in brown fur that smelled of damp earth and mold, appeared, peeking out from behind the trees. She caught a glimpse of something long and shiny, sliding out of a massive black shape. Its head appeared to be covered in wet moss and was too small for its body. Sarah did not see any eyes. Each time the creature moved, she tried to make out another part of its shape, but it eluded her. Only the smell was tangible, pervasive; a mixture of fur, earth and mold. Its hot breath smelled of rotting meat left out on a summer day.

*** 

Sarah woke with the stench of the creature still prevalent from the dream. The sun was beginning to rise behind the mountain range. She took a few deep breaths of the fresh morning air, and with each waking minute the terrifying dream faded from her memory.

After a light breakfast of bread and cheese, Sarah packed up her camp and continued on with her mission. By midday, she and Jacob reached the outskirts of the Perquot village. The modest encampment was enclosed within a circular wooden barrier which acted as protection against outside invaders. Only one narrow passageway led into or out of the camp.

As Sarah made her way through the opening, she could hear the buzz of life—children playing, women singing, and the sound of heavy lifting as men shouted instructions to one another. It wasn't unusual for the Perquots to have outside visitors, but they were most often men in packs of two or more. Rarely had a lone woman entered their camp. A child spotted Sarah and ran up to her in amazement. The little girl tugged on Sarah's leg, bright eyes wide with excitement. The child's mother followed her gaze and was the first to notice Sarah. She stopped what she was doing and ran to tell the elders of the stranger.

The entire village grew quiet as more eyes focused on Sarah. After several long uncomfortable minutes, one of the elders she had met before in Wysterfield, came out of an ornamented wigwam at the center of the village. His name was Woyowooit, and he had a striking presence with broad shoulders and a lean, muscular physique. As he approached Sarah, she could feel the power and influence emanating from him. But his eyes—once she looked into his eyes, she saw a peace and knowingness. It put Sarah at ease.

As she climbed off Jacob, she approached the chief with a bow and handed him the freshly baked bread she brought as a gift. Woyowooit nodded in response and, upon accepting the bread, showed her to his wigwam. Once inside she heard the life outside resume its steady hum.

Woyowooit spoke to her. "You are the first white woman to enter our village."

Sarah was impressed by his English. "Thank you for allowing me to break bread with you, Chief Woyowooit. I have come on my own seeking guidance and answers to the terrible things that are happening in my village."

"Ah, yes, your people have already come and asked me about this. I will tell you what I told them. You bring about your own destruction." He said this without emotion.

"I do not understand. Do you know what is killing our people?" Sarah asked, puzzled.

"What has killed those people is of your own making. Our people believe that bad things will happen to bad people. Honamock has come to your village because there is something that he wants."

"Honamock?" asked Sarah.

"Honamock is death to our people. He is a spirit that can slide onto the mist, invisible to all, save his prey. At night he comes and feeds on souls." The chief took a breath then continued, "We who are with the Great Spirit have nothing to fear from Honamock. It is only the treacherous with evil in their hearts that can lure Honamock out from his slumber. Your people have awoken him, and he is hungry after so many years. Many moons ago, our people suffered greatly at the hands of the Honamock. My father's father's father was then Chief Sasacus, and he was corrupted with greed and power. He wanted all of the land and the fertile fields for himself. He set out on a war path against all the surrounding tribes, killing the men and taking their land along with their women and children. The blood he spilt on the land awoke the Honamock. In the quiet of the night, the Honamock grew stronger and preyed on those in the village. As the ancestors tell us, there were never any warnings of Honamock. Only what he left behind."

"And what was that?" Sarah asked.

The chief bowed his head and shook it from side to side. "He left no trace of the people who once were. He ate their souls, leaving only broken bodies. Each night he would slaughter entire families. This went on for several nights until it finally ended. The Honamock took the soul of the corrupted one, the dark one, Chief Sasacus. Once his soul was devoured, the killings stopped."

"But how did your people know it was the Honamock that killed the villagers and not an animal or another villager?" Sarah asked.

Woyowooit raised his head and looked Sarah in the eyes. "Your people do not know the difference between the natural world and the world of spirit. For our people, they are one and the same. We know what comes from Mother Earth and what is of Father Spirit. We know when the wind blows from the great mountains that a storm is coming. We know when the harvest is good that the Great Spirit is with us. We know that when illness befalls us, our spirit is out of balance with the Great Spirit. We know the difference between animal, man and spirit. Do you? Your people see but are blind to the world, blind to the Earth, blind to the Sky. We are one with all."

Sarah sat stunned, not sure how to process what she just heard. *He too believes a devil has come to Wysterfield. But why? What did the*

*Garretts or Goody Mary do to incur his wrath?* She had so many questions swirling around in her mind, but no words left her mouth. The chief stood and gestured to the door, and before Sarah knew, she was back on her horse and riding out of the settlement.

\*\*\*

The journey back to the village was tedious. There seemed to be an increase in debris on her path as Jacob carefully navigated through the broken branches and tree stumps. She felt on edge and thought she heard footsteps following her, but when she looked back she saw nothing. She returned to the village the next day, after stopping for only a few hours of rest.

The village was full of activity. Sarah sensed frenzied energy and saw worry on a number of faces. She stopped Goodman Isaiah.

"What is the matter?" Sarah met his wide stare.

"You haven't heard? Young William has taken ill. He has lost his pallor and can no longer speak."

William Glenhock III was the reverend's youngest son; a small, curious boy who loved playing in the woods, and capturing tadpoles and dragonflies along the stream. He was not yet eight years old.

The news startled Sarah back into the present. She realized her mind kept replaying the words of Chief Woyowooit. Sarah returned Jacob to the stables and set out towards the reverend's home. A handful of townspeople gathered out front, and Sarah heard wailing from inside.

As she approached, Glenhock emerged, wiping blood from his hands on a white cloth. "Friends, my boy has gone to be with the Lord. For he was too precious for this world, too perfect, and God came to take him." Tears streamed down his face. "His mother and I were only caretakers to him, looking after him until it was time for him to return to his heavenly home. Please give us time to mourn in peace." The reverend retreated back into his home, closing the door behind him.

As if guided by an invisible hand, each member of the village slowly returned to their respective homes. Not a word was spoken. Not a question asked or an answer given as to what befell poor William. Sarah found this odd. Still standing in front of the Glenhock's home, her keen ears heard the boy's mother wailing behind the closed door.

\*\*\*

Later that evening, as Sarah was preparing her supper, a knock came at the door. It was Goodman Nicholas, the town's unofficial peacekeeper. There was little need for a peacekeeper in a village this small, but when Goodman Matthew took too much ale or when there was a dispute over some trade, Goodman Nicholas was the one the villagers went to for resolution.

"Forgive the intrusion into your supper, Goody Sarah." Nicholas entered, removing his hat.

"You are always welcome into my home, Goodman Nicholas. Would you care to break bread with me?" Goody Sarah pulled up another chair and quickly assembled another plate of food for her guest.

"You are too kind but I am only here for a minute. Can you tell me where you were the last few days? Goody Lydia mentioned that you went to gather seed. Is this true?" he asked while taking a seat at her table.

"Yes of course, that and I wanted some time away from the village to clear my head. I cannot make sense of all the death that has plagued our community over the last few weeks. What do you make of it?"

Goodman Nicholas simply looked past Sarah and shook his head, his eyes a dull haze, out of focus. "I wish I knew, Goody Sarah," he said. "I have not slept in a fortnight. I do not understand what is happening. No man can explain what has taken place. I have spoken to each household and cannot decipher the cause of it. And now with little William meeting his Maker, it is too much."

Sarah saw in his eyes the glistening of a tear.

Regaining his focus, he said, "Tell me, when you left the village, did you see or hear anything along your journey? Anything that might explain what has been happening here?"

"No, I am afraid not. It was just Jacob and I on the trail. I heard but an owl and saw neither beast nor man." Sarah kept her visit to the Perquots to herself as women were not allowed to visit with anyone outside of the village. She knew Goodman Nicholas to be a fair and just man, though she did not always agree with him. Still, she did not feel the need to share her excursion with him.

"I found some hearty Indian corn upstream about a day's journey out. I grabbed what I could along with some spinach and parsley I found along the trail. I hope to include it in my garden next spring," Sarah added for good measure.

Goodman Nicholas seemed to not hear her. "Well, I am glad you made it back safely. Had I known you were venturing out I would have advised you to stay close to the village. We do not know what is upon us, and I mean to keep everyone safe from harm —especially you, Sarah." And with this he raised his head and looked her in the eyes. She had not noticed before, but there was a genuine look of concern on his face. He stood hastily, placing his hat back on his head. "Good evening, Goody Sarah, please be careful and do not venture outside of the village again."

***

The morning light was a welcome sight as Sarah's nightmares corrupted her sleep. This time little William joined Mary and Margaret as their twisted and deformed faces taunted Sarah with bulging eyes. Sarah's body shook itself awake. Drops of sweat poured down the sides of her temples, as the fall air stabbed at her with its bitter cold.

"I will find out what is plaguing our community, I will," Sarah said out loud in her empty cabin. She arose with determination and a fortitude she had not experienced since the death of her love,

Robert. She was determined to find the answers the others failed to see. Sarah gathered her supplies and locked up her cabin once more. She mounted Jacob and rode off to the outer rim of the village, to the deer stand set up by the hunters in years past. This modest wooden structure was elevated some eight feet off the ground and bordered the forest. It had two small, square openings, one facing the village and one facing the forest. It was here, during the fall months, that the hunters would take turns scouting the fields for deer and other wildlife. With fall turning into winter, the shack stood empty with little save the four walls, ceiling, and floor to keep out the elements.

Sarah hitched Jacob to a nearby tree and set up the hunting shack for her surveillance. From this vantage point she could see anything coming in or out of the village. She was determined to know what was causing the deaths, whether it was the Honamock as the Perquots believed, or the work of man. As morning turned to afternoon, she could hear the hum of the village below. No one would miss her, as all would still be in shock over the loss of the reverend's son. There would be no call to church today.

Sarah ate her lunch and contemplated what she would do if she did encounter whatever was hunting the villagers. She had brought Robert's musket with her. She took it out and inspected it, taking it apart and cleaning it with purpose, as Robert had shown her years before. The gun had been given to Robert by his father, and it was now one of Sarah's most treasured possessions: a small reminder of her beloved husband.

She carefully poured the black powder down the barrel, followed by a lead shot, and ensured there was enough powder in the flash pan. She released the safety from half-cock to full, and was ready to fire if the call arose.

Afternoon turned to dusk, and dusk turned the skies to a pinkish hue which faded gradually to indigo as night fell. Sarah gathered her garments and drank her coffee from earlier that day. She did not risk lighting a fire; she did not want to alert anyone or anything to her presence. She placed the barrel of the gun through the small opening facing the forest. She braced herself for the cold and kept a keen ear out for any movement.

As her eyes adjusted to the dark, she glimpsed mice, possums, and other night time creatures scampering across the forest floor searching for food and shelter. As the moon rose directly above the village, a tightening spread across Sarah's her neck and shoulders. The sounds in the forest grew silent. A frigid wind blew through the structure, forcing Sarah to shield herself from the cold. She looked out onto Jacob, who seemed equally alert and silent.

The air began to change. It grew thick and dense, making it hard for Sarah to breathe. A wave of heat suppressed the night air, as if a fire were burning nearby. Then came the smell. It was the stench of Sarah's dream that night, alone in the forest, of decay and death mixed with wet fur and earth. Sarah dry heaved uncontrollably as the odor hit her nose. It was unlike anything she had ever experienced before. She nearly dropped the musket but kept it steady, ready to light the fuse. Her insides screamed at her to run—but she sat still, focused on her task.

A vibration rose up from the platform as if something enormous were moving towards her. The makeshift shack shook in each corner, forcing the wooden slats to groan. Sarah felt alone, vulnerable and exposed. She gathered her musket and peered into the forest, searching for any movement.

As the stench grew stronger, she lit the rope fuse of her musket and placed her finger on the trigger. Jacob broke free of his reins and galloped back towards the village. Out of the mist, a dark circular shape started to swirl directly in front of her. It materialized from the ground up—widening its frame into a funnel, spinning like a hurricane as it picked up leaves and twigs in its wake. It grew to the size of the shack Sarah was in. She could not make out the trees behind it. It was the deepest black she had ever seen. No light penetrated its surface. Two wiry arms sprouted out from either side of the blackness like tree branches. Spider-like hands with sharp, metallic fingers protruded from the arm stumps. The long, silvery fingers reminded Sarah of sewing needles. She counted eight writhing from each hand. The moonlight glinted off the fingers as they opened and curled, independent of each other. Sarah heard a scraping sound like the sharpening of a knife. Then finally, terribly, the head emerged. A mustard-rimmed ring with a jagged edge appeared, its center a void like the rest of the body. Two more identical rings grew within the first until there were a total of three. The yellow rings quivered, birthing pointed obsidian teeth. Each ring spun at different rates, the one in the center spinning with the greatest velocity. The series of teeth gnashed at the open air. The remainder of the head, too small for the rest of its broad body, formed with a mixture of earth and moss and what looked like mangled fur from a fox or squirrel.

Sarah fired her musket directly at the creature and it transformed into mist. A hot rush of putrid air hit Sarah as the Honamock spirit blasted through the shack, heading towards the village. She fell backwards both from the backfire of the musket and the force of the Honamock. Then all went black.

*** 

Sarah awoke to the sound of screaming coming from the village. It took several long minutes for Sarah to grasp what she had witnessed. Her mind was on the verge of breaking, feeling less tethered to reality. Screams again shook her back into focus. She grabbed her musket and made her way out of the shack and ran back towards the village. Firelight came from the town center. The townspeople were moving towards the blaze, and as the church came into view, Sarah saw it was alight, with flames on all sides.

The townsmen were frantically carrying water from the well to try and put out the fire, like ants using the dew on a leaf to put out an inferno.

*Impossible*, Sarah thought, as the flames licked high into the sky, shooting upwards as if reaching for heaven itself. A loud creaking sound broke through the crackling of the fire as the mighty church bell came tumbling down, no longer supported by its wooden frame. The bell hit the ground, sending an earthquake across the village with enough force that Sarah's feet and knees quivered. She looked around and surveyed the chaos, when she noticed an object at her feet. It was square with rounded edges, and a series of etchings coated its surface. It looked familiar but she could not place it. As she bent to pick it up, she noticed it had a metallic sheen to it, with an eerie similarity to the Honamock's needle-like fingers. It had some weight and a green glow about it. As Sarah held the object, a warmth enveloped her hand. It did not look like stone or metal; it was something altogether unfamiliar. Then it hit her: this was the reflective object she'd seen in the well months ago, just before the killings took place. The townsmen must have brought it up inadvertently when drawing water to put out the fire. She felt lightheaded with the object in her hand, and nearly fainted as the scene around her changed.

Sarah was no longer standing in her village. She was in another time and another place, deep in the forest. She stood outside an enormous cave, one large enough to house the entire village. She saw only blackness inside the hollow and felt the warmth of the Honamock closing in, accompanied by its decaying smell. A man approached the cave. As he drew near, Sarah recognized him as Reverend Glenhock. She called out to him, but he did not see or hear her—and she realized what she was seeing had already taken place.

She watched as he entered the cave, returning moments later with a shiny object: the same one Sarah now held. As the mirage in front of her faded, she saw yet another image, this time the reverend was joined by Deacon Josiah and Goodman Zachariah. All three stood naked around a fire. Sarah witnessed markings on their bodies, cuts and bruises and what looked like blood smeared across their chests.

Sarah looked into Glenhock's eyes and saw a fury she had not noticed before. A wildness, deranged and yet focused on the task at hand. He spoke.

*"Great Honamock, I demand you come and whet your thirst. I have something of yours—your lifeless heart—wake and do as I command!"*

The others moved around the fire, screaming and hooting like animals consuming their prey.

The scene changed once more, and Sarah saw Glenhock speaking with Goody Margaret, alone.

*"You are so beautiful, Margaret. Goodman Richard does not deserve you. The Lord spoke to me and told me you are a daughter of Christ and must be anointed by his appointed servant. I may be so blessed as to bestow upon you God's gifts."*

Before finishing his words, Reverend Glenhock was upon Goody Margaret, raping her in her own home, her boys watching from a corner.

Sarah, unable and unwilling to see what was before her, fell to her knees in anguish. She let out a guttural scream, one filled with anger and disgust. Before she could take another breath, the scene changed once more, and she was transported to the morning her friend was murdered. While getting the breakfast ready for the family, a gray and black mist entered the cabin through the cracks in the home; through the doorframe, around the windows, through a few loose floorboards, from the ceiling above. It was as if a fire on the outside had enveloped the house and now the smoke was seeping into the interior. Goody Margaret hadn't noticed, but her twin boys were fixated by the sight.

As the mist gathered inside the cabin, the same shape Sarah had witnessed moments ago formed. It stood behind Goodman Richard, seated at the table awaiting his breakfast. The creature forced its needle-like fingers into Goodman Richard's mouth, the only sound heard was the cracking of his jaw breaking as the fingers expanded. Once the creature had located its intended target, the fingers retracted—and with them came a pink v-shaped piece of tissue: Goodman Richard's voice box. Blood dripped down the creature's metallic arms. It tilted back its grotesque head and fed the tissue into the inner circle of teeth.

Goody Margaret grabbed her two sons and pulled them close to her, as if trying to pull them back into her womb for protection. It was of no use. Within a breath, the monster's fingers broke into

Goody Margaret's mouth, breaking her jaw and retrieving the same pink and bloodied tissue as her husband's, rendering her voiceless. Then with the precision of a surgeon, the creature repeated the same procedure on the twins simultaneously, one set of fingers in each mouth. Again, the monster tilted its head back and with a sucking and slurping sound, fed the tissue into its innermost mouth.

What came next would forever fill Sarah's mind with nightmares. With each member of the family still alive and unable to utter a sound, the creature slowed its pace. It went back to where it started, to Goodman Richard. The Honamock stretched its upper body until it reached the ceiling. The creature bent over Goodman Richard's body, the three rings of teeth beginning to rotate and spin, each ring moving in opposing directions. It placed the innermost ring of teeth directly over Goodman Richard's left eye. Four black fangs emerged from the four corners of the ring, hooking onto Richard's face like anchors. The sucking, slurping sound returned, and in what felt like far too long, Richard's left eye was pulled out of its socket. Then came the right eye. Once done, Richard's body fell motionless onto the table, his outstretched hand pointing towards his family.

The creature jumped onto the boys next. Margaret tried to push their heads towards each other to protect them, but it was a futile effort, the Honamock was already upon them, sucking at each until their eyes bulged out of their sockets like their father's. The boys then slumped back facing each other, lifeless.

Last came Margaret. Sarah witnessed the sheer and utter terror in her friend's face, but also something else. Knowing her family was gone, there was a hint of relief that Margaret would soon be joining them. With Margaret, the creature seemed to revel in its task. It took twice as long with her as with the other members of her family. Its back shook with what looked like excitement as it sucked at Margaret's eyes. Then Sarah heard a horrifying *popping* sound. Margaret's left eye had detached and hung loose on her cheek. Then the same was done with the right. Sarah's friend

FRANCESCA MARIA

slumped forward, her head towards her children, eyes on her cheeks, the last of her breath sucked out of her. The creature stood back and shrank into its original shape, as it dematerialized back into mist once more, leaving the cabin through the cracks.

Sarah, frozen with fear, dropped the object she had been holding and was transported back to the fire in front of her. She fell to her knees and retched the sticky residue from her coffee a few hours before. She lifted her head enough for the dizziness to set in, then collapsed, unconscious.

Goody Sarah awoke to the sound of Goodman Nicholas yelling her name, "Sarah! Goody Sarah! Are you alright? What has happened?"

"I am sorry, I must have fainted." Eyeing the shiny object on the ground, Sarah quickly picked it up and concealed it in her front apron pocket. "I am well. It is just a shock to see the church aflame. So many hours spent in the Lord's house. So many memories, all lost now." Goodman Nicholas helped Sarah to her feet.

"We do not know what started it. Perhaps a cat knocked over a candle left burning?" Goodman Nicholas did not sound convinced. The structure was now burnt to the ground, with a few remaining support beams refusing to give up their station. A small cyclone of fire shot straight up into the sky, past the height of the trees of the forest. "It seems so unnatural," Goodman Nicholas said, staring at the remaining flame.

"Was anyone injured?" asked Sarah.

"Goodman Elizar had a beam fall on his leg. I do not know the extent, but he suffered severe burns as others tried to free him. I know of no other injury." Goodman Nicholas spoke in a whisper, as if to show respect.

"I am sorry to hear that. What of Reverend Glenhock and his family? Were they able to escape the fire?" Sarah's heart raced at the thought of him.

"Yes, they escaped. They seem shaken but uninjured. They are at Deacon Josiah's house." Goodman Nicholas pointed towards the

30

deacon's home, despite it being a village of not five and twenty structures.

"Well then if you will excuse me, I would like to see if they are in need of assistance." As Sarah took her leave, Goodman Nicholas held onto her arm.

"Wait, let me accompany you. There is something that does not feel right and I do not want you walking alone."

Sarah did not protest, only nodded, and the two walked in the direction of the deacon's household. She was unsure of what she would do when she saw Glenhock. She felt the Honamock's heart weighing down her pocket.

The entire village had gathered now that the fire was out. They stood outside the deacon's house, adjacent to the church remains. Some of the townspeople were more vocal than others, crying out to God for his mercy and questioning why such horror had befallen their quiet village. Sarah heard whispers as the eyes turned in her direction.

Goodman Nicholas cleared a path for them as they made their way towards the deacon's front door. The townsmen stopped Goodman Nicholas, asking him what he thought was the cause of the fire. A great many wanted to find the culprit, the devil lurking among them. Distracted by their questions, Goodman Nicholas did not notice as Goody Sarah continued onto the deacon's home alone.

Sarah approached the door, and it swung open. Standing in the doorway was Deacon Josiah, holding a bloody handkerchief over his head. He did not see Sarah and nearly slammed into her on his way out the door.

"Oh! Goody Sarah, forgive me, forgive me! I did not see you there," Deacon said without care. He pushed Sarah to the side and walked right past her into the waiting crowd outside.

Sarah peered into the home. The good deacon's wife Charity was comforting Agnes, Reverend Glenhock's wife. They were lost in each other's tears, and did not notice Sarah as she walked through the door. Goody Sarah locked onto Glenhock, pacing the small enclosure, muttering to himself. His eyes had the same crazed look as in her vision.

As Sarah approached, he shook himself back into reality. "Ah Goody Sarah." He greeted her with a false smile. "It is a sad, sad day. Our beloved church, the one my father, the beloved Reverend William Glenhock Senior, built with his own two hands … it lies in a puddle of ashes. And this so soon after losing our beloved William to the Lord."

At the sound of her son's name, Goody Agnes let out a cry of sheer agony.

"Come, Goody Sarah, let us discuss this away from the grieving women." Glenhock took Sarah's elbow with force, and led her out of the house through a back door leading into the woods. The loud cries from the crowd were still audible as she and the reverend retreated further into the trees.

"It is so good of you to come, Goody Sarah. Since our boy grew ill, Goody Agnes has not allowed me to touch her as a husband. You are good to offer me your comfort at this time." Glenhock reached out to caress Sarah's face. She recoiled at his touch and backed away from him a step, clutching the object in her apron pocket.

"I know what you did!" Sarah screamed. "I know what you did to my friend Goody Margaret and her family. I saw what you did to her!" She did not realize she was shaking. Her screams were not heard over the crowd on the opposite side of the house.

Glenhock's eyes hardened as he took in Sarah's face. He did not say a word.

"I saw you leave the cave with this!" She pulled out the talisman from her pocket, brandishing it in front of him. "And I saw you summon the Honamock! You are a monster! *You* are the one who has set this evil upon our village!"

He grabbed Sarah's arm with a force that frightened her.

"How did you get that? Where did you find it?" he demanded.

"It must have been pulled up when the well was drained for the fire. When I held it, I saw visions of what you had done. You are an evil, evil man! How could you do that to Goody Margaret? How could you unleash that monster on her boys?" Sarah was in tears, but her anger and fury would not let her break.

"Ah, Goody Margaret, yes, her skin was sweeter than mother's milk, and her taste of morning dew." Glenhock looked off in the distance, reminiscing his conquest. "I do not relish her demise, but she had threatened to tell her husband and the elders of the village. She had already confided in Goody Mary, so I had to send the Honamock to pay the old woman a visit." His eyes were focused on Goody Sarah once more. "And the inverted crucifix on her chest, I added that. I thought that was a nice touch. It added great magnitude to my sermon. That day I was as good, no, *better* than my father at the pulpit. I had finally come into my own, no longer standing in my father's long shadow. And the deacon here"—he pointed towards the house—"acquired that nice plot of land owned by that cow, Goody Mary. What use was all that land to her with no man to till it for her? Such a waste—but not anymore! Only, the beast came after my son … my poor innocent boy. I caught it standing over him, draining his soul. Once Honamock has awoken, its thirst knows no bounds." Sarah's confused expression fueled Glenhock's fervor as he hung onto her arm with an iron grip. "Oh, you do not know what the Honamock desires, do you? Well let me ask you this, Goody Sarah, what does the Good Lord say is the window to the soul? Hmmm? Do you remember your Sunday school teachings?"

Sarah shook her head.

"No? Well then, let me tell you. The window to the soul is the eye, for it is the eye that sees the light of God and the eye that sees death as it approaches. The Honamock sucks out souls through a person's eyes. Oh, and it loves to feast on souls, especially those that are pure and full of God's light."

The reverend laughed; his grasp on Sarah's arm tightened, causing her real pain.

"So when the beast came after my son I threatened the Honamock. I reminded the creature that I alone controlled its actions, for I knew where its cold, dead heart had been hidden."

Sarah looked horrified at the object still in her clutches.

"Yes, that's right; you are holding the heart of the Honamock. I hid it at the bottom of the well and only used it when I needed the creature to do my bidding. The Honamock hissed at me, but then slithered back into mist and left—but by then the damage was done. My perfect son's jaw hung broken, his eyes bulging. He could not scream. He could not cry. He just sat in his bed beating at himself until his heart gave out the next morning. My wife was inconsolable, and still is." Tears ran down the sides of the Glenhock's face.

Trailing off, Glenhock acknowledged, "The beast must be gaining strength. I saw its shadow smash into the church windows, knocking the candles in its wake. It has come looking for me, for what you have in your hands. But now I must find another hiding place. First, let's see if you taste as sweet as your friend, Goody Margaret, shall we?" He pulled Sarah deeper into the woods. As Sarah screamed, another voice entered the night air.

*"Reverend Glenhock! Reverend Glenhock! You are needed!"*

Deacon Josiah ran to the two of them in the forest. Glenhock released his grip on Sarah, only to hand her over to the deacon.

"I have found the witch! I have found the witch! Bring her to the front of the church where she will face her God!" Reverend Glenhock was renewed with a fresh plot.

Deacon Josiah dragged Sarah behind Glenhock as he made his way back to the crowd still gathered at the ruined remains of the church. Sarah screamed and protested but it was of no use. Deacon Josiah placed his other hand over her mouth to quiet her.

"God-fearing people of Wysterfield," screamed Glenhock, "we have witnessed a plague upon our town! Goody Garrett's family, Goody Mary, my poor boy—all dead! Killed by a demon that hides among us! And now, our own house of God, the one my very own beloved father built, has been burned to the ground. I say unto you, this cannot stand! The Devil might come but we will always cast him out, for the just, the righteous that live with the Lord in their hearts will always overcome darkness."

Gesturing to the deacon, Glenhock spoke once more. "Bring her here, Josiah."

Facing the reverend, Sarah noticed a smile form on the edges of his lips.

"We, good people, have a witch among us! I saw Goody Sarah with my own two eyes set the church aflame! She is the one who has unleashed the Devil upon us! And she has confessed to me her dealings with the Devil, for once I placed the good book of the Lord upon her chest, she spat her confession as it was forced from her! She told me she saw visions of an evil creature stalking among us! That she was the one who summoned this demon to our town for her own amusement!" Goodman Nicholas moved towards Goody Sarah. Deacon Josiah stepped between him and the reverend. Glenhock grabbed Sarah fast by her hair which was now hanging loose from under her bonnet.

Not wanting to give the crowd an opportunity to ponder this newest accusation, Reverend Glenhock shouted, "Thou shalt not suffer a witch to live!" He bent down and whispered to both Deacon Josiah and Zachariah, his co-conspirators in the woods that night. They went to the church and together grabbed a support beam that the fire had spared. They stood it on its end, and found another beam to secure it, then fashioned a makeshift bonfire at the base with the remaining wood. The deacon disappeared inside his home, emerging with a series of ropes.

Goody Sarah pleaded her case. "No! It is Reverend Glenhock who unleashed the Devil, the Hona ..." Sarah trailed off as Glenhock struck her hard on her face, knocking her to the ground, stunning her into silence. Deacon Josiah and Zachariah bound Sarah's arms and legs together with the rope, then fixed her to the support beam just feet from the smoldering church.

The stunned crowd gathered in front of the burned churchyard. Goodman Nicholas was the only one who protested. Once Goody Sarah was secured to her fate, the two men went to hold down Goodman Nicholas.

"For those who feel sympathy for this creature"—the reverend pointed towards Goody Sarah—"show sympathy for the Devil himself! There is no fire hot enough to cleanse the wickedness from a witch. There is nothing that a man can do to right the wrongs of the Devil's making. No, only God and the Devil himself can settle this score. Light it!" he commanded.

His two co-conspirators set the pyre ablaze. Sarah's senses were renewed as her lungs struggled for air amongst the thickening smoke. She could hear the sound of Glenhock's voice, condemning her to the pits of Hell. With her bound hands, she reached into her apron pocket and squeezed hard on the Honamock's heart, piercing her flesh. Her blood poured out onto the creature's heart. A mist formed behind the reverend. The outstretched arms of the Honamock reached forward, embracing him from behind. The last thing Sarah heard was the sound of the esteemed Reverend Glenhock's scream. As the first flames began to catch onto the hem of her skirt, Sarah smiled.

# SHANE O'REILLY

There is a place in Ireland, just beneath the mountain of Errigal in the county of Donegal, where rolling green hills and sheep outnumber people. It was upon these hills that a man by the name of Shane O'Reilly made his living shepherding his livestock amongst the cold, hard stones of the mountain. O'Reilly was born working and hoped to die the same. He lived alone and kept to himself most days. His hands were as rough as his manners and he didn't much care for outsiders. That's why, when the Dark Man came to his village, O'Reilly wanted nothing to do with him and kept his distance.

At the end of a long day's work, all the locals gathered at the pub and discussed the affairs of the hour. It was on one of those typical days that the Dark Man entered the pub. A tall and slender figure, with shiny black hair that hung at his shoulders, he had a way about him that was altogether foreign.

The smoke in the room parted as the stranger chose a seat at the far corner of the bar. Once the townsfolk had taken in the man's countenance, they carried on with their local chatter. Not O'Reilly. He sat at the far end of the bar facing the Dark Man. He did not like this man. Not one bit. The Dark Man's long, black coat gave him an air of treachery as if he were hiding something beneath the folds, and his longer face told O'Reilly he was no part of the Isle.

"Humph. Foreign pig," O'Reilly said under his breath, quiet enough so no one could hear, not even the bartender—or so he thought. As he finished uttering the phrase, the Dark Man turned his full attention towards O'Reilly. And before O'Reilly could finish his thought, *what's he staring at*, the Dark Man slid onto a stool next to him.

O'Reilly hadn't seen the Dark Man take one step towards him. He shook his head. *Must be the drink*, he said to himself. One moment the Dark Man was in the booth across the bar, the next he was practically breathing down O'Reilly's neck; studying him with great care.

"Oy!" shouted O'Reilly. "How did you get 'ere so fast? And back up a bit, aye? I'm not looking for company."

"Forgive me," the stranger said, speaking in an accent O'Reilly couldn't quite place. "I am new to this town, and was looking for a friendly face to show me around." The stranger grinned, sending a wave of ice through O'Reilly's body.

"*Humph*, friendly." O'Reilly chuckled. "Either you're as drunk as I, or you're half-blind! I am *not* the welcoming committee. You can just as soon go back from where you came from as far as I'm concerned."

In that moment, Shane O'Reilly realized something different about the stranger. Something he hadn't put his finger on until now. His eyes had no whites. They were all black save for a hint of blood red around the edges. It gave O'Reilly a start as he reflectively recoiled. There was something else, something not quite right with this stranger—he had no smell.

Every man, woman, and child O'Reilly ever encountered gave off their own unique scent. A baby had the smell of its mother's milk; a farmer, the sweat of the day mixed with the animals he tended. Everyone in that bar, everyone O'Reilly had ever met, had their own smell—except for the Dark Man.

O'Reilly moved to get up, but the man raised a hand and motioned for him to sit back down. The stranger's fingers were long to match the rest of him, with uncut nails that were eerily transparent. O'Reilly looked at his fellow patrons, hoping they'd catch his eye—but he was frozen to his stool, unable to even turn his head.

In a flash, O'Reilly felt a piercing pain in his skull, as if someone were stabbing a protracted, thick needle through the top of his head. He felt the tip wiggling around between the two hemispheres in his brain. He lost all ability to move or speak. There was just the pain, followed by the voice.

*"You will show me your village, Shane O'Reilly."*

As soon as the voice left his head, O'Reilly and the Dark Man exited the pub, walking along the same path O'Reilly had walked hundreds of times before. Still unable to speak, O'Reilly guided the visitor to the five-room farmhouse he called home, to the barn where he stored his feed and supplies, to the fields where he kept his livestock. At each place the stranger simply nodded, as if in agreement with a statement that hung unuttered in the cold evening air.

After passing a series of farmhouses, each similar to the one before it, they came upon a small cluster of buildings in the town center. All of the buildings were identical, save for the signs out front which gave them each a name: Roarty's Place—a small store that served as a shop, post, café and (once the Open sign flipped to Closed), a pub; Megan's Cottage, which housed the occasional and rare traveler; and the Dunlewey Center, which was a meeting place for the landowners to handle local disputes. O'Reilly showed the Dark Man what was once the Dunlewey Church, high up near the mountain's edge. The church was nothing more than a shell, abandoned by man, ruined by nature.

A sly grin appeared on the Dark Man's face as he surveyed what was left of the once-hallowed structure. O'Reilly thought the man seemed to marvel at its demise.

They walked back towards the town center. A stone's throw past Roarty's Place was a modest cottage tucked off the main road, hidden amongst the rolling hills. The Dark Man stopped and lifted his nose to smell the air, seemingly mesmerized by the nondescript abode.

"Who lives there?" asked the Dark Man.

"Why, that's the McGeady's home, or what's left of it." O'Reilly was surprised to hear the sound of his own voice. The temporary control over his vocal cords had been lifted. "No one lives there save for Abigail, the youngest daughter of Brendan. Once her parents died, she took over the place. Her brother Paul moved to the city once he got outta university, let's see, that must be o'er ten years ago now."

"We must go in," commanded the Dark Man.

"But it's getting late. I don't think she'd appreciate two men showing up on her doorstep at this hour. Plus, you're ..." O'Reilly hesitated, catching his words in his mouth. "A stranger."

"But you are not, Shane O'Reilly. Come, let us meet this Abigail McGeady."

The whitewash of the home gave it an eerie glow as the moon rose higher up into the sky; a disregarded bone in a sea of the deepest blue. The porch was plain, with two rectangular windows, closed with thick curtains, and a heavy wooden door.

Before O'Reilly could knock, the door opened and there stood Abigail in her nightdress, a past beauty now showing age, her auburn hair draped in a plait over her shoulder. She looked dazed, as if awoken from a deep sleep.

"Greetings, Abigail, I am called Adolosam, at your service." The Dark Man bowed low with grace and ease.

O'Reilly stood frozen once more, unable to move or utter a sound. He stayed outside the door as the Dark Man made his way into Abigail's home, shutting the door behind him.

O'Reilly stood helpless, unable to hear anything on the other side of the door. He thought of countless unspeakable things the Dark Man could be doing to Abigail. There, the unlucky O'Reilly stood all night, unable to move even a fingertip. Unable to control his bladder, he pissed himself twice. The first time his urine was warm; the second time, it was cool.

As dawn approached, breaking the darkness with a yellow glow, he felt his extremities again. First his right toe, then his left. Then his forehead loosened, next his hands, until slowly, painfully, he regained control of every muscle and tendon.

When the sun was properly over the hills, he was able to take a step. It took all of his effort and concentration to move, stiff as he was from standing all night. After several excruciating minutes, he was able to reach out and open Abigail's door. As he turned the knob, he caught the smell of something metallic, familiar, and yet he couldn't quite put his finger on it. Was it copper?

The small cottage was dark, save for a few slits of morning sun from a backroom window. As he took a step forward, his foot landed on something wet and sticky. He knew in an instant what that smell was—blood. As his eyes adjusted in the darkness, he saw the entire wooden floor covered in a thick layer of blood, more than he thought possible from a single human body. He called out to Abigail, praying for—and yet fearing—a response.

*"Abigail?"* His voice was barely a whisper.

He sloshed deeper into the front room, darting his eyes back and forth, searching for any movement.

"Abigail?" he repeated, this time with more volume, but with a quiver in his voice. He heard an odd sound from the back room. He took one step after the other, willing himself to move. He still felt half-frozen but whether from the Dark Man's control or his own fear he could not tell.

He approached the room with a sickening in his gut, and thought he would lose control of his bladder once more. The sound grew clearer and louder as he approached. It was now a slight gurgling noise, as if sucking liquid through a straw.

Abigail, or what was once Abigail, sat up in her bed, her ravaged neck exposing windpipe and cartilage, her nightgown now a darkened red. Her skin was so white, so pale that Shane scarcely recognized the warm, cheery neighbor who would sell him her homemade pies at the harvest fair.

*"Abigail,"* O'Reilly whispered.

With this utterance, Abigail's head lolled to the side, looking O'Reilly straight in the eyes. The eyes that met his own were milky white pools floating on a sea of red.

O'Reilly had not realized his legs had given out on him. He was surprised to see himself on the floor, kneeling at the foot of the bed. As he staggered to get up, still unsteady on his feet, he collapsed again on the slippery floor, landing face down in Abigail's excrement, pooled under the bed.

Slipping again as he raised his head, O'Reilly screamed a guttural sound, one he had never before heard cross his lips. He gathered his feet a third time, and as he did so he heard something behind him.

Adolosam stood in the doorway cleaning the corners of his lips with a red handkerchief, which he then tucked with care into his sleeve. Without looking at O'Reilly, Adolosam uttered, "I very much enjoyed meeting Abigail. She was quite a stunning creature. Now, Shane O'Reilly. You will take Miss Abigail McGeady out to the pasture behind her home to the yew tree. You shall bury her standing upright with her head facing the earth, six feet, nine inches down. Then you will set her home ablaze and meet me on the high hill outside of the village at sundown."

This was not a request. O'Reilly, in his horror, could not fathom what was being asked of him. He sat in silence.

"Now," commanded the Dark Man.

As soon as the word was spoken, Shane O'Reilly's legs took on a life of their own and lifted him off the ground. Once more, he felt that intrusive prick in his skull, inching further down between the two lobes of his brain. Though the pain was blinding, O'Reilly was not able to utter a sound.

As O'Reilly went about his gruesome task, the Dark Man disappeared. O'Reilly spent the entire day digging the ditch then carrying Abigail's body, wrapped in her blood-soaked bed sheets, to her makeshift grave under the yew tree.

As the sun was high above his head, O'Reilly felt hunger set in. Unable to stop for rest let alone food, he felt faint, then started to hallucinate. Shapes and colors merged and melded through the sweat in his eyes. With Abigail's body still wrapped in her bed sheets beside the grave, O'Reilly could have sworn he saw movement from out the corner of his eye. At one point—perhaps because of his digging, perhaps because of the process of decomposition—Abigail's pale white hand reached out from under her cocoon, motioning for O'Reilly.

He tried to scream, but no sound left his lips. The smell of her corpse decomposing in the afternoon sun mixed with his empty stomach. O'Reilly dry heaved, and found he could not open his mouth. He nearly passed out as he hyperventilated through his nose.

At one point, he thought he heard his name in the wind, called in a faint whisper: "*Shane O'Reilly.*" Never stopping, never ceasing, his limbs worked on their own accord as O'Reilly remained imprisoned within his own body.

The hours ticked by and the hole started to take shape. By late afternoon, O'Reilly had reached the desired depth. He climbed back out, dirt and bits of earthworm black beneath his nails. He carefully rolled Abigail's linen shroud into its grave. The body landed face down with a thump, twisted and bent. Once more, O'Reilly thought he heard his name called out, this time from within the grave itself. Terror filled his eyes as he shoveled dirt bit by bit, covering the thing that was once Abigail. Several times he could have sworn he saw the linen move as the dirt hit its surface. Still, he kept shoveling. Several more hours passed until the grave was filled and all that remained was a patch of fresh earth beneath the yew tree.

He set about his next task of burning the McGeady's home. From within the makeshift shed attached to the back of the home, O'Reilly found a can of kerosene used to light the oil lamps. He grabbed the canister and a box of matches from one of the cabinets.

He expected to see others out in the village. He prayed someone from the town would come to his rescue and free him from the control of the Dark Man. O'Reilly coated the back of the house with the kerosene. He then went inside and grabbed all the flammable linen and furniture his body could carry, and piled it up against the fuel-lined wall of the house. The smell of blood mixed with petrol again caused O'Reilly to heave. He was still unable to open his mouth, and thought for sure this time he would suffocate.

His body seemed unaffected, or unwilling to admit that its owner was in full revolt. The body moved deliberately with purpose, methodically taking one step then another, commanded by the Dark Man.

As O'Reilly set the house ablaze, he wondered about his own fate. What was to become of him, Shane O'Reilly of Donegal? Would the Dark Man kill him, too? Would he end up in a grave like Abigail? Would he be forever trapped within a body that he could not control; performing further unspeakable acts for his new master? Would he welcome death as sweet relief from what lay ahead?

Shane O'Reilly contemplated this as he walked towards the high hill of Errigal.

# MY BROTHER ANDY

We never talked about the haunting in our house, at least not until we were adults. Witnessing my bedroom closet opening on its own accord became one of my earliest and most pervasive childhood memories. My sister Anna remembers sharing the room with me, and watching my terror as I learned what she had already discovered about the thing in the closet. Before I came along, she had been in that room, alone, for six years. She knew quite well that something lingered in that closet—but she never dared talk about it. The strange occurrences in our house intensified over time: closed doors rattling, scratching sounds from inside the walls, whispers under the bed, footsteps in the attic, toys coming to life.

Many of my scariest experiences happened around age seven. I frequently found myself trapped in the downstairs bathroom. When I'd try to open the door, the handle jammed and wouldn't budge, trapping me for what felt like hours. Something I couldn't see or touch attached itself to my back and breathed hot air on my naked skin. I panicked, crying and screaming for someone to come to my aid. Eventually one of my parents would hear my cries and rescue me.

The doorknob had a simple push-button lock with no key. It puzzled my dad as to how it got lodged so many times; he would have to unscrew the doorknob from its base and remove all of the components in order to set me free. He replaced that doorknob over a dozen times. To this day, I still don't understand why it only targeted me in the bathroom. My oldest sister, Terry, had a bedroom upstairs in an isolated part of the house. Her room scared me the most because it bordered the attic.

The upstairs consisted of a large family room that led into Terry's bedroom which is where we'd access the attic. It covered half the upper floor of the house. Like most attics, ours consisted of a haphazard storage space filled with Christmas decorations, old clothes and games that we had outgrown. To get anything in or out of the attic, we had to climb down through a makeshift corkboard door in Terry's room. The door closed with a simple hook latch, but this did not prevent it from opening on its own. Once through the door, we had to then skillfully balance and climb across the narrow wooden slats of the unfinished floor.

One false step could plant a foot right through the ceiling of a downstairs room. The attic was in the shape of an L, with the bottom of the L outside of view. There were two windows facing out into the street, letting in just enough light to see where we were going and cast enough shadow to make us feel like we weren't alone. We would often hear footsteps and wind whipping through the attic, despite it not having a floor and the windows were sealed shut.

Terry described a scratching on the other side of the corkboard much like what we experienced downstairs. But unlike our closet, she heard something on the other side of the door—knocking. We avoided that attic instinctively, knowing that whatever was haunting us each night had made the attic its home. Terry took no joy in sleeping next to the attic door night after night. She'd make our dog, Dusty, sleep with her and she'd play her Rolling Stones or Who records all night and sleep with the lights on so she wouldn't hear or see whatever roamed the attic.

My mother and father were in complete denial about what happened in our childhood home. My mother, a devout Catholic, dismissed anything paranormal because it went against her beliefs. My father, a stoic and practical man, didn't believe anything he couldn't see, hear or touch. When he heard my sisters and I discussing the odd experiences we encountered, he rolled his eyes.

"That house wasn't haunted, it was all in your imagination," he'd repeat.

I could buy this perhaps, if what happened to my sisters and I turned out to be the complete story. But how could we explain away what happened to my brother? He was only a child, for chrissakes. His experiences were, by comparison, more terrifying than the rest of ours.

*** 

My little brother Andy, the youngest of my parents' brood and the only boy, had a room adjacent to mine and Anna's. My parents' room was down the hall from us, close enough to see if we had our lights still on, but far enough away to not be able to hear the noises coming from within our walls.

When Andy turned seven, he started experiencing things in the house for himself. Before then, he'd grown into a happy, friendly kid. He loved playing sports with football quickly becoming his favorite. He belonged to the local Cub Scouts, where he learned everything from basic first aid to how to survive in the wilderness. Andy turned out to be a great kid, fun to be around and a loving brother and son.

All that changed after the first attack.

What happened to my brother took place when I was thirteen and he had just turned eight. The story I remember is pieced together from fragments of memory aided by a retelling from my sisters, several years after the family had moved out of the home. During a blustery winter night, a tree branch sliced through a power line, leaving us in the dark. Our parents took this as an opportunity to send us all to bed early. I remember having trouble sleeping that night as the wind shook the bushes against my bedroom window.

I awoke to a bloodcurdling scream coming from Andy's room. My mom and dad thought that someone might be trying to break into the house—they ran into my brother's room, looking for the source of his terror.

They found nothing, except a horrified young boy who sat clutching the sheets as if they were a protective shield. My father asked Andy what was wrong.

"Something grabbed me," Andy forced between tears.

"It was just a nightmare, Andy," my father replied. "Go back to sleep."

This had become my father's typical response. My parents shooed my sisters and I to our rooms, and went back to bed. Andy tried his hardest to forget what happened and went back to sleep, unaware of the danger he was in.

Andy woke again, this time, he would tell us later, to something cold and wet grabbing at his ankle in a vise grip, paralyzing him with its hold. As the hold tightened, a low, gurgling noise that sounded like a laugh filled his bedroom. After what seemed like an eternity, the hold on his ankle subsided. The house roused again to Andy's screams. This time when my parents went to investigate, they noticed something odd. They scrambled to switch on a flashlight, and saw Andy's sheets had been completely shredded. The entire lower half of his sheet, from his knees down, had been ripped—though his outer blanket remained untouched. My parents were baffled, and assumed Andy must have ripped them himself with his toenails while having a nightmare.

For countless nights after that first event, Andy would wake up with a new terror; his sheets were pulled off the bed or were wrapped around him so tight he couldn't breathe. Or he'd have the same experiences that had paralyzed him on that first night. Once, he described being woken up by a hard slap on the side of his face. And after each occurrence, a low, muffled laugh would pulsate through the room. Each time my parents dismissed it as either an overactive imagination or an attempt to seek attention, Andy being the only boy in a house with three older sisters. I wanted to protect Andy and keep him safe. But there was nothing I could do to stop what was happening to him.

Soon after his nightly terrors began, Andy started to change. Instead of being the outgoing Cub Scout and rambunctious brother, he started to withdraw. He often preferred to sit in an isolated part of the house by himself rather than in the living room with the rest of the family. He became unstable and angry, and prone to sudden outbursts. The changes were not only psychological, but physical too. Andy would steel himself up, preparing for the next night's battle. We saw him physically change as he pumped up his chest and clenched his muscles, psyching himself up for what lay ahead each night.

He told me later he would check the closet and under the bed before climbing under the bedcovers. Sometimes he'd steal my mother's holy water and sprinkle it around the perimeter of his bed, hoping to ward off any evil spirit. On occasion, he would go so far as to sneak out of his room and find lodging elsewhere, or not sleep at all. We would often find him watching television in the morning, claiming to have been there all night.

Each night, night after night, came a new fear. This continued for years until my older sisters, Anna and Terry, left home for college and Andy decided to move into the now vacant upstairs bedroom. All seemed fine for the first few nights. Andy even seemed a bit more cheerful. My brother made the room his, putting up posters of bands he liked: Black Sabbath, Judas Priest and AC/ DC, to name a few. Having the much-feared *attic* room didn't seem to bother him. In fact, he seemed perfectly content in his new surroundings. Weeks passed with no terrified screams in the middle of the night, and it appeared Andy had finally put that awful time behind him.

Unfortunately, the peace was short-lived.

Late one fall night, there was a knock on my bedroom door. The noise jolted me out of a deep sleep, and as I shook myself awake, the knock came again, this time followed by a shy,

*"Hey Jessie, you awake?"* Andy's voice sounded much younger than fourteen.

I turned on my light and opened the door to find my little brother, pale and shivering with eyes wide and the most horrible look on his face.

"It followed me upstairs," Andy whispered.

"Who? What are you talking about?" I tried to comfort him but I saw the look on his face and how terrified he was.

"No, you have to believe me. It ..." He hesitated. "It ... wants me."

At that point he broke down, and I sat him on my bed. He started to cry and shake uncontrollably.

All at once it became clear to me. Deep down, I knew what he was talking about—I'd had experiences of my own. The fear I had been carrying around gave way to a new terror. In an instant I knew the thing which had trapped me in the bathroom was real. It wasn't my imagination. The rattling of my closet doors wasn't from the wind. The guttural, gurgling noises I heard from under my bed weren't from a dream. The footsteps in the attic weren't the house *settling*. With immediate clarity, I knew the truth. We had all been living with a secret: there was something else in our house.

"It's going to kill me," Andy whimpered.

"No Andy, it's not going to do anything to you. I won't let it." I grabbed my robe from the foot of my bed and took his hand. "Wait here," I told him, not believing the words coming out of my mouth. "I'm going up there." I squeezed his hand and left the room.

Looking back on that night now, I wonder why I didn't tell my parents. I guess I didn't want to be told again that it was all in my imagination, or to simply *go back to bed*. I remember feeling pissed off that this thing had made my younger brother, now almost a man, cower and weep. As terrified as I felt that night, I had more anger than fear—and I let that propel me forward.

I felt my way through the hallway into the darkness. By the time I reached the foot of the stairs, a rustling sound greeted me from the top landing. I felt as if it were daring me to go further. A shadow moved across the top of the stairs for a second, and then it was gone.

The noises and rustling continued, increasing the closer I climbed to the top of the stairs. Our dog, Dusty, whined from the bottom of the stairs, as if pleading with me to not go any further. I almost conceded, but then I remembered Andy, my little brother, sitting in my room, shaking like a child. No, I had to keep going. For him and for myself.

Once at the top of the stairs I crossed the family room and headed towards Andy's bedroom, nearly falling over beanbag chairs and musical equipment. As I reached the bedroom door, I started to feel that same hot breath that had surrounded me in the bathroom creep up behind me. My body shivered involuntarily, as if trying to shake off whatever had encroached on my personal space. My breath grew shallow as some invisible force squeezed my chest. I seized the door handle with both hands and jerked it forward. Nothing. I tried again: still nothing. The door wouldn't budge, even though there were no locks on the door and there was no one in that room. Well, no *one*, but some*thing* was.

The family room became frigid, making my breath visible in gray puffs. I desperately wanted to run back down the stairs and out of the house forever, but that was no longer an option. I'd be afraid all of my life, and Andy would never be able to recover if no one faced what he faced, if no one truly believed him.

I tried the handle once more, this time with success and little effort. It was as if the bedroom now invited me in. Stretching, as my hand turned on the light, I caught a glimpse of something black move before the bulb burnt out with a pop and darkness prevailed again.

The black shadowy form glided from Andy's closet to and through the attic corkboard door. Droplets of sweat dripped down my forehead into my eyes, and ran unencumbered down my back. A *thump, thump, thump* pounded from the other side of the attic door. I don't remember what ran through my mind at the time or what I had planned to do. My only objective had been to confront it, whatever it turned out to be.

Feeling my way against the wall, using Andy's posters as my guides, I reached and grabbed onto the narrow frame of the attic door. With trembling hands, I moved down the frame until I found the latch and lifted it off its perch. Another thump. Icy cold air pushed its way into the room as the door opened. The two windows on the west end of the attic cast an orange hue from a streetlight, allowing for some light to invade the darkness. More thumping erupted from the unseen part of the L in the attic. Looking down for where to place my feet I recognized the familiar Christmas decorations we'd be pulling out again in the next few months. That seemed so far away, like another life altogether not my own.

Holding onto the doorframe with both hands, I lowered myself down onto the attic floor. In the darkness, I struggled to locate the first wooden slat, and landed instead on the soft padding, nearly puncturing a hole through the floor. After regaining my footing on a plank, the sound of a familiar, low gurgling reverberated in the empty space. Peering into the darkness, I spotted a shadow forming from the corner of the room. It appeared, seemingly, out of nothing. As it grew, the gurgling sound morphed into a deep, sinister laughter. Paralysis came then, seizing my lower extremities. I couldn't move and barely drew breath, bound by some unseen force. I felt trapped and vulnerable, just as I'd been in the bathroom countless times before.

The only distinguishing feature in the shape appeared to be an arm-like extension, with what looked like a fish hook at the end. The mass kept moving up and down and side to side as if it were weightless, being tethered to the ground by an invisible string. It made a scratching sound, like sandpaper as it moved, creating friction within itself. The smell of sulfur and a chemical like nail polish wafted from the being. The head of the entity—I guess you could have called it a head—consisted of lit charcoal, burnt black with gray around the edges and no distinguishing features, except for the eyes. The eyes glowed a fire-red that pierced through my skull. It spoke to me telepathically, causing my being to shudder with pain.

"He's mine," it said with authority. "His innocence will feed my thirst."

"*No*, you can't!" I shouted, pushing the words out of my mouth. "I won't let you have him!"

"Silly girl, you're too late" the thing hissed.

Then, in an instant, it moved from out of the corner and towards me with incredible speed, lifting the contents of the attic in the air as it did. Boxes of Christmas decorations, clothes, and board games flew across the room, spilling their contents onto the attic floor.

I tried to scream, but the air got sucked out of my lungs as the force knocked me down onto my back. I remember losing consciousness and waking to find the entity hovering over me with its hot breath and fiery eyes searing through me.

"He's mine now, girl. It's over. He's mine ..." The being laughed, a terrible, maniacal laugh. How can a laugh, an expression of joy, be corrupted into something so sinister?

The creature vanished. I screamed like I'd never screamed before: a long, loud, guttural cry. The sound of movement from downstairs quickly followed my father calling my name. Footsteps came up the stairs. The attic door swung open.

My father lifted me from the bottom of the attic floor and kept shaking me, hoping I'd wake from the shock. The only thought that permeated my mind was that I had lost; it was too late. Then it hit me. Andy! I had to go to Andy.

Jumping out of my father's arms, I ran down to my room where Andy lay, sitting up, smiling at me with a grin that did not fit the Andy I knew. The entity had been waiting for me.

"It's all right, sis, I feel better now. Much better," it said with a low gurgling voice.

***

Years passed. We never talked about what happened that night. My parents wouldn't have believed me anyway. Eventually, they sold the house and moved out to the country. My older sisters and I married and started families of our own. And Andy, well, Mister Abrams, you probably know more than I do. Andy was never the same. My sweet, fun-loving brother got swallowed up by the entity that night. It possessed Andy, taking full control like a puppet master, causing nothing but loss and devastation in its wake. The string of robberies and assaults occurred when he hit his late teens and early twenties. Then he got an acquittal for the attempted murder of that family of four. After that, Andy disappeared.My sisters and I tried to find him and get him help multiple times over the years, to no avail. It wasn't until he was arrested last fall that we had any indication that he was even still alive …

\*\*\*

"Thank you, Ms. Jager, for your account," Mr. Abrams said, feverishly scribbling notes in his yellow legal notepad. "You've been very helpful."

"Do you think this will help his case? The Andy I knew would have never hurt anybody, let alone a whole family like that. Didn't I read in the news reports that they were found in a bathroom locked from the inside? And each one had been brutally dismembered, even the little baby?"

"I am not allowed to discuss the details of the case, Ms. Jager."

"It was that thing, that night; it stole my brother away from us. It's the one that committed those murders, not Andy. Please, you have to believe me."

"We'll do everything we can to convince the jury of that, Ms. Jager, but it won't be easy. 'The devil made me do it' is not a defense tactic that I think will award your brother his freedom. But we will have psychiatric evaluations done to determine if he was in the right state of mind when he murdered the Olsens. The fact is, all of the evidence points to your brother as committing the murders, or, at the very least, having a heavy hand in the crime."

I left the courthouse distraught and exhausted. I hadn't talked about that night in such detail with anyone before. I've tried to forget about what happened, every day for the last twenty-three years.

The Detention Hall sign pointed me towards the south side of the marbled halls. I wasn't sure what I'd say, but knew I had to see him. I needed to look him in the eyes and determine if Andy was still in there or if my brother truly died that night in the attic of our childhood home. The guard checked my ID, made me sign a form, and waved a wand over my body. "Follow the yellow line to the door marked 'Visitors' and wait in the chair on the left."

I nodded at the officer and made my way down the yellow line. The chair faced a thin Plexiglass barrier with a phone hanging on my left. I stared at the fingerprints and stains left on the plastic divider and waited for Andy.

I barely recognized him when he came through the prison door. He looked much taller than I remembered, and darker. Not that his skin was darker—his features were darker, like he'd been dunked into a vat of tar. I don't know quite how to explain it. His beautiful, strawberry-blonde hair had turned jet-black along with his eyebrows and facial stubble. His upper body, once fit from exercise and sports, hung loose from his shoulders, appearing lanky and sinewy. His torso seemed out of proportion with the rest of his body—longer and narrower than his lower half. I noticed his eyes last. Purplish gray half-moons curved under his eyes.

"What's up, sis? What are you doing here?" it replied, the voice unrecognizable over the prison phone.

"I came to see you. I told the lawyer everything, everything about that night." I hesitated, reverting back to that fearful young girl, lowering my gaze. "I know it wasn't your fault. It's that thing, that entity made you do it." I lifted my head from the table and looked him in the eyes. And in an instant, I knew. I knew what I feared all along as I stared across at those fiery eyes.

"Don't you fret one bit, sis. It's okay. I've got him."

Ignoring my fears, I placed a hand on the Plexiglass and stared back at the creature. "Andy, if you're still in there somewhere, I'm so sorry and ..." holding back tears, "I love you."

A low chuckling arose from the being in front of me. It stood and placed both its hands on the glass to meet mine. The laughter grew into a loud rumbling causing the Plexiglass to reverberate in protest. It opened its mouth into a wide gape and screamed at me, "He's mine!"

I dropped the phone and ran out of the prison, never looking back.

# THE PERFECT PARTNER

Marissa had been waiting for her visitor to arrive for over a month now. Waiting, longing for its presence each night as the sun set. The last experience had left her agonizing for more.

*Would it return?*

*Could they do it again?*

Somehow, she knew that tonight, with the full moon, it would be back. She turned off the water and dried herself. She unwrapped her new silk teddy, the one she'd purchased for her special friend. The fabric made her skin come alive, caressing it like a gentle kiss.

Marissa moved to her bedroom and shooed her cat off the bed. It squealed in protest, but she ignored it. She opened the curtains, revealing her back porch, and unlocked the sliding glass door. She lit candles in each corner of the room, then turned off the lights. The incense she'd been burning left a pleasant, subtle smell of gardenias in the air. She pulled back the covers and lay down on the sheets. Marissa waited and waited, until her eyes grew heavy and she glided into sleep, dreaming of a mysterious hand caressing her face.

As the moon rose high into the night sky, Marissa awoke to the sound of her picture frames rattling against the walls. Her bed shook, sending vibrations through her prone body. The half-spent candles trembled and their tiny flames flickered, casting miniature shadows across the room.

*He's here*, she thought to herself.

She saw the old, familiar bright light from her back porch; a seductive grin filled her face. The back door opened, and feet shuffled into her bedroom. In less than a breath, there stood the creature that had sent her insides soaring so many times before. The cat looked up from its sofa retreat, unimpressed, and fell back to sleep with a lazy purr.

Marissa sat up. "I've been waiting for you to return."

The creature gave a nod and proceeded to the side of her bed. It raised its pointed chin and closed the deep black pools of its eyes. Marissa opened her mind.

"I know that you wanted me to return."

She loved how it could penetrate her mind without spoken words. She was beginning to understand how to use telepathy herself.

She replied, "Come to me, Bakari."

Without movement, the sheets left her body. Invisible hands played under her teddy. One grasped her right then her left breast, and caressed them—covering them each with invisible kisses. Hands worked to slide off her panties, and she helped by lifting her hips then her legs into the air. By now, more hands removed her teddy and she lay naked in complete rapture. Her thighs were spread open and fingers moved up her legs. Unseen tongues worked in her ears, her mouth, across her nipples, her thighs, between her legs. All the while, Bakari remained motionless with his head poised as before, his eyes closed. She knew what would come next.

With great care, Marissa was levitated until she hung in mid-air, a few feet above her bed. Suspended in the air, she felt as if she were lying on a bed of clouds. The invisible tongues and hands on her body moved with a heated fervor. With her legs pried open, Marissa felt gushes of air enter inside her. Massaging hands grabbed her hips and her backside, opening her even more.

Marissa felt hands, then wrists and arms, as the invisible form took shape. She felt a torso, shoulders, legs and feet on top of her own as her lover solidified, still unseen to the eye. She arched upward to greet it. The being caressed her face, her breasts, and gently lay on top of her, seeping into her flesh. She felt the chest becoming a part of hers, the legs intertwining with hers. The thick, warm appendage searched for her opening.

Penetration.

Marissa locked with her lover as they circled and spiraled in the air with ease. Hot breath moved up and down her neck and face; the back of her head braced gently against an invisible shoulder. Marissa gasped as faint grunts emanated from her chest, and the rhythm of their lovemaking reached a crescendo. Marissa climaxed as her lover's appendage surged past her inner walls, through her insides and up her spine. They hung, motionless except for the pulsing of her orgasm. Her body filled with goose bumps and a warm heat. Her invisible lover kissed her then disappeared. She was lowered back to her bed and placed under the covers.

Bakari dropped his chin and opened his eyes. "Thank you," he said without speaking.

"Thank you, lover. Come again soon," replied Marissa.

"I will," promised Bakari.

Marissa heard feet shuffle back to the porch, and saw the lights fade into the sky as she drifted off to sleep.

# THE CIRCUS

Joey wasn't going to miss the circus this year. He had missed it last year due to Boy Scouts, and the year before that because it fell on his little brother Stevie's birthday.

He loves it when the circus comes to town. It's run by clowns; everyone from the ticket taker to the acrobats under the big top are clowns. There are sad clowns, happy clowns, funny clowns, scary clowns, all with different expressions painted on their faces. The one thing they all have in common is their big red lips, bright red, the color you'd see after someone gave you a pink belly. Joey loves the clowns; he thinks they are the best part.

The circus has carnival rides like the Tilt-A-Whirl that makes you sick and others that go upside down. It has games with cool prizes like an oversized stuffed animal, or a plastic gun that explodes with a flag at the end when you pull the trigger. Behind the games is the House of Mirrors. It's a walk-through maze of mirrors of all different shapes and sizes, followed by a short boat ride through a cave where the mirrors and low lights cast shadows on the water. It's where bigger kids make out, much to Joey's disgust.

One year, Joey dragged his little brother Stevie into the House of Mirrors—but they exited immediately because Stevie wouldn't stop screaming. He kept saying he'd seen something staring back at him through one of the mirrors.

\*\*\*

The circus came to town one day a year: on the last Sunday of September, just as the leaves were beginning to turn. This being that fateful day, Joey arose early and raced his bike over to his friend Timmy's house so they could watch the crew set up the big top. Joey was old enough now to go places on his own—not too far, though. By the time he and Timmy pedaled their bikes to the vacant lot, they were shocked to see the circus already set up and fully operational, including all the rides and flashing lights. In fact, they were able to buy tickets and go in if they wanted. Joey couldn't figure out how they'd set up the circus so quickly. There was no sign of it anywhere yesterday. It was like magic.

Timmy didn't care; he was already in line, ready to buy his ticket. His bright blue eyes, wild with anticipation, scouting out all the circus had to offer. He wanted to ride the Bone Crusher, a pretty accurate description of how one felt after riding it.

Joey reached for his wallet, and realized he hadn't gotten his allowance yet. His parents usually gave him money on Sundays, and in his haste, he forgot to ask for it a day early. As he peered in, he found a crisp twenty-dollar bill tucked neatly in the back. The surprise hit him, where had it come from? His wallet was empty the day before when he tried to buy a pack of gum from Wendells. Maybe his mom put it in there before he left.

At the ticket booth, the boys were greeted by a forlorn-looking clown with deep, shadowy eyes and a long, droopy grin. The clown didn't say anything, just pointed to the sign that showed 'Adults $15, Kids under 14 $8'. The boys got their money out and handed it to the clown whose name, according to his name tag, was Virtue. Virtue gave them their change then pointed them to the turnstiles, never saying a word.

Timmy ran right up to the next clown, this one with a happier demeanor, named Charity, who eagerly took their tickets, tore off the stubs, then motioned them to enter. This clown didn't talk either. They made their way to the Bone Crusher and Timmy was first to line up. Another clown with a furrowed brow and an angry frown ushered them onto the ride. His name tag said Temperance.

The ride lived up to its name, and Joey started rubbing his neck as soon as they disembarked. Timmy wasn't at all fazed; few things could slow him down. Joey didn't think Timmy had noticed that none of the clowns talked. It was super strange, like their mouths were sewn shut. But there didn't seem to be any thread, just those bright red lips.

The boys got on and off the various rides before the place started to fill up with other eager kids. By lunchtime they had ridden everything three times: the Tilt-A-Whirl, the Giant Centipede, the Atom Smasher and of course, the Bone Crusher. The only thing they didn't ride was the House of Mirrors, which had an 'under construction' sign posted out front. At high noon, a big gong chimed and a funny voice over the loudspeaker invited everyone to take their seats inside the big top, the show was about to begin!

Once again, they were greeted by mute clowns and shown to their seats by more clowns who also somehow lost their voices. Joey wondered if they were supposed to be like that mime guy he saw in the park when they were on vacation. That guy dressed all in black and white, and pretended he was trapped in a box and wouldn't say anything. Joey guessed some people found it funny, but he found it weird.

Joey was amazed to see how many people were already in the big top. It didn't look that crowded when they were walking around outside. Where had all these people come from? Before he could finish his thought, the lights went out—and one single spotlight lit up the center of the stage. Out came a massive, shiny clown covered head to toe in bright-colored sequins, complete with a top hat, white face and a huge grin that went from ear to ear. He was standing on a little red wagon, wheeled out by a tiny monkey riding a tricycle and dressed like a clown.

"Ladies and Gentlemen, Kiddies and Creatures! Welcome to the Circus of Righteousness, where we find out who are the virtuous and who are the wicked! Who will rise to the great gates of Heaven, and who will perish into the fiery pits of Hell? Let's see, shall we?"

The Ringmaster bellowed out a voluminous cackle that made Joey squirm in his seat. Loud music started to play; circus music, but slightly off. It sounded like when Joey hit a wrong key in piano practice. It was almost right but sounded wrong somehow.

Out came the first set of performers. One was a female clown with a frilly gown, holding a dainty umbrella over her head. The next was a clown dressed in a black suit, with a big mustachio. He kept getting closer to the woman (who, on closer inspection, was a man dressed as a clown dressed as a woman), and every time he advanced, he twiddled the ends of his mustache, and she giggled and moved further away. If she sat on a bench, he'd follow her. She'd move over to the other end of the bench, and he'd get closer. She'd get up and move to a tree, and he followed. And so on. Joey didn't quite understand what was going on, but the mustachioed clown was funny and kept tripping and falling every time he got near the woman clown. After a while, the female clown ran off backstage and the mustachioed clown followed her, tripping on his pants which fell down as he started running. The crowd erupted in laughter.

There was silence for a little while, and darkness as all the lights turned off. Joey was starting to feel uncomfortable, just as the center stage light came back on, and under it appeared two small children dressed as clowns. They couldn't have been Stevie's age, they were too small. They looked disheveled, dirty and sad. There was a little tin cup in front of them, and they each held a sign. One read 'Will Work for Food' and another said 'Donations Please'. A few feet away, the spotlight turned onto a well-dressed clown wearing a fancy suit with polished black shoes and a top hat. He looked wealthy, like he owned Wendells or something.

The dapper clown whistled as he walked, and once he spotted the children, his eyes narrowed. He reached into his pocket and jangled a whole bunch of change right in front of the clown children. He pulled out a big polished gold coin, grabbed their tin can and dropped it hard into their cup. When he did, the other few coins in the cup jumped up to the surface along with his gold coin. He grabbed his own back, and placed all the other coins into his pocket. He gave the children back their empty tin with a tip of his hat, and walked on, still whistling his tune without skipping a beat.

The clown children looked stunned as they peered into their empty cups. Neither said a word.

The lights went out again, and through shadows, an enormous platform was wheeled out from the left of the stage. It made a squeaking noise, as if the wheels themselves were protesting the weight. As the lights came on, Joey could see how gigantic the platform was—it could fit three grand pianos, like the one his music teacher had. The makeshift stage was pulled by a gigantic gorilla; the kind at the zoo, that beat their chests when they get angry. The gorilla wore a red fez hat with a black tassel that hung over his eyes, a sequined blue-green vest that barely fit, and his eyes looked meaner than mean.

The platform was kind of hard to make out at first, the way the lights shone down on it. As it moved closer to the center, a gargantuan clown appeared. The clown was naked, save for a blue-green sequined cloth draped over his groin. Smears of sweat ran down his painted face, making the colors slip and slide. Joey thought the clown must have been at least six or seven hundred pounds by the look of him.

The behemoth sat eating buckets of chicken, one after another, all the while making disgusting slurping sounds. Joey thought he was going to be sick. The clown sat there eating for another ten excruciating minutes before he was finally wheeled offstage. In his wake he left a dozen candy wrappers, three empty chicken buckets, four large soda bottles and a dirty rag. A small monkey in a clown costume came up behind him with a broom, and pushed the trash offstage.

This was like no circus Joey had ever been to before. He didn't remember it being like this in years past. It was weird and made him feel uneasy. He figured there was something adult happening that he didn't understand, which happened a lot for a kid of nine. The adults were always laughing at things that Joey didn't find very funny. Like now, some of the adults were laughing and clapping. Timmy was unusually quiet sitting next to Joey, staring at the emptied stage with his mouth wide open.

Once the stage was cleared, the house lights came back on, and rows and rows of clowns came out from everywhere, converging together into the main ring. Soon dozens of clowns filled the stage. Some clowns were juggling, some were getting little dogs to walk on their hind legs, some were taming lions in a corner, another was riding a giant elephant.

It was all very loud and noisy and chaotic. Joey didn't know where to turn his attention—then he noticed the same clown that had spoken in the beginning. He was in the very center of the stage, on his red wagon, moving his arms to and fro like an orchestra conductor. He was smiling, with his head looking up into the tent lights like he was in a daze.

Just as everything was escalating, the lights abruptly went out, and stayed out. After a few minutes, a handful of people, unclear if the performance was over, timidly started to clap. A dozen more joined in until the house lights came on, showing an empty stage. The exit signs lit up, indicating it was time to go.

Joey was more than a little disturbed at what he'd seen. He thought the animals were cool, but he didn't understand the rest. It made him feel funny inside—almost dirty, like he should be ashamed about something. Timmy didn't seem fazed by anything. He kept talking about the big gorilla and *"Did you see how fat that guy was?"*

When they made their way to the exit, they were surprised by how dark it was.It felt as if they had been in there for maybe an hour, but outside it was well into night time. Timmy tugged at Joey's arm. "Look, they opened the House of Mirrors, let's go!"

The House of Mirrors flashed with alternating blue and white lights, a stark contrast against the deepening night sky. The entrance was a wood carving of a massive clown face with a gaping mouth, framed with blinking lights.

"No, I better not. I'm supposed to be home before it gets dark. My mom's going to kill me if I'm not back in time for dinner," Joey lamented. "You go on ahead."

The friends parted ways. Timmy ran towards the entrance of the ride, and Joey retrieved his bike and made his way back home alone.

***

Monday morning came around, as it always does, and spoiled a perfectly good weekend. Joey grabbed his backpack and headed off to school. He found himself thinking back to the circus. Why didn't any of the clowns talk except for the ringmaster? Why did they have such funny names, and what were those little skits about?

During roll call, Joey noticed that Timmy was absent. Joey was disappointed—he'd wanted to talk to his friend about the weirdness of the circus, and ask him about the House of Mirrors. He'd have to wait until tomorrow.

After school, as Joey rounded the corner with his bike, he noticed a patrol car parked in front of his house. He had never seen a police car in his neighborhood and the sight of it in front of his own home made his heart skip a beat. He parked his bike and saw his mom gesturing for him to join her through the open front door. A man's voice mixed with his mom's as he entered the kitchen.

"Joey, this policeman would like to ask you some questions." She leaned on the kitchen counter.

"Hi Joey, my name is Officer Land and we've been looking for your friend Timmy. He's been missing since last night. Do you know where he is?"

"No, sir. The last time I saw Timmy was when he went into the House of Mirrors, at the circus."

"Did anyone approach you and Timmy while you were at the circus yesterday? Did anyone talk to either of you?"

"No, um … No one talked to us the whole time we were there."

The officer thanked Joey. His mom told him to wait in his room while she finished up with the policeman. A few minutes later, she came into Joey's room and explained that no one had seen Timmy since he left for the circus on Sunday morning. He never returned home that evening. Timmy's parents had been looking for him all night, but thought (or rather, hoped) he had just wandered off on his own and would come home when he got hungry or ran out of money. Timmy was the kind of kid who got distracted easily. Like the one time he was coming home from school and saw a fox that he followed until he got lost in the woods behind the baseball field. It took hours to find him and he had no sense of how long he'd been gone. But despite his wandering tendencies, Timmy wouldn't stay out on his own overnight. He wasn't *that* dumb.

\*\*\*

When the police inspected the circus grounds, they found that it had already packed up and cleared out. There was no trace of the circus anywhere, not a stray candy wrapper or ticket stub. The lot was completely empty. No one knew where they were headed or how to get in touch with them. The police pulled the circus's permit, and traced it back to an Apotropaic, LLC Corporation. When researched, this turned out to be an empty and abandoned warehouse in another city, in another state. There was no sign of any business ever being there—just rats, dust and decay. The police hit a dead end.

\*\*\*

Flyers went up around the neighborhood. Timmy's parents appeared on the local news, pleading for their boy to return home. Search parties went out every Sunday. No one had seen or heard from Timmy since that fateful night.

\*\*\*

The next year rolled around, and there was no circus. It skipped Joey's town that year. Sometimes that happened, when dates conflicted with other events. Still, it was odd when they didn't show up again the following year either.

By the time the circus came again three years later, Joey was well into his pre-teen drama with puberty pushing his hormones into high gear. And this time, the circus was in a new location, a few towns over. Timmy had become a distant memory. Everyone assumed the worst: that he had been taken by some creep on his way home from the circus. Joey tried to not think about it. It made him feel sick to his stomach.

Joey asked the girl with the flowing blonde hair in his math class, Clarissa, to go to the circus with him. To his surprise, she agreed. When the last Sunday of September came around, they met up at the park and together rode their bikes the rest of the way to the big top. Joey felt uneasy being there again, but he couldn't tell if it was because of his lost friend or his overactive hormones. When they got to the ticket counter, Joey pulled out his wallet to pay for them both. A clown pointed to the ticket price sign without saying a word. Joey noticed something about this young clown, whose name was Patience. The painted smile looked forced, out of place next to the strained clown's forehead. His smile was too wide and his face too youthful, for such a furrowed brow. His deep blue eyes locked onto Joey's. They were wild and urgent and yet somehow familiar.

Before Joey could make the connection, Clarissa pulled him through the main gate, straight to the House of Mirrors.

# The Legend of the Chupacabra

Why do we tell bedtime stories? Is it to instill fear? Is it to keep us safe? Or is there a deeper reason lying just beneath the surface of our collective consciousness? Could there really be ghouls and goblins lurking in the dark recesses of our civilized society, or are they figments of our societal imagination? Or perhaps, maybe, we tell them because they are true.

Take for instance the Legend of the Chupacabra. This roaming dog-like goat sucker has been seen ravaging livestock for generations. But what is it? Where did it come from? Let's listen in on the tale of the Chupacabra …

***

Grandfather pulls up a chair near the crackling fire, and gazes into the stars. He breathes in the night air and his eyes glisten at the sight of his grandchildren playing around him.

"Gather close, *niños*. Let me tell you the story my grandfather told me of the Legend of the Chupacabra."

The grandchildren, ranging in age from three to eleven, assemble around the fire, eagerly awaiting the tale.

Grandfather began. "Many thousands of years ago, when the earth was still covered in ice, food and shelter were scarce. Animals had to adapt and adjust to the world, or perish beneath the weight of it …

***

One day, unable to find any food, a lone wolf was on his last dying breath. He wandered into an ice cave resigned to his fate. As he prepared to take his final breath, he heard the flapping of wings above him. The great wolf raised his head with tremendous effort, and saw a gigantic, leathery bat swooping down towards him. The wolf, too weak to fight him off, simply showed his teeth with a low growl.

"Do not bare your teeth at me, great wolf," said the bat, "for it is of no use. I smell death upon you. You have not long to live."

The wolf raised his giant head and with a snarl replied, "Well I'm not dead yet, you foul thing. Leave me to die in peace, then you can have your feast."

"You mistake me for an enemy," said the bat. "I come to you as a friend. I believe we can help each other."

"I have nothing left to give," the wolf replied. "I have not seen an elk or bear or any other creature, and thus have not eaten in four moons. I cannot survive another day."

"That is where you are wrong, my friend," said the bat. "I can gift you life eternal, where you will only need one thing to sustain you."

"What do you mean? What is this that you speak of?"

"Blood," the bat answered.

"You are absurd, and I must be imagining this."

"Oh no, I'm quite serious. I can grant you life eternal, where all you would need is a few drops of blood to sustain you for four *hundred* moons." And the bat moved ever so slightly closer to the wolf.

"It is not possible." The wolf lowered his head again. "What do you seek for this thing you are offering?"

"Warmth," explained the bat. "I can no longer sustain my life energy in this cold world. Soon I will also perish without the means to sustain my internal warmth."

The shadowy bat looked down upon the wolf with its piercing red eyes. "You, great wolf, have a thick coat of fur and warm blood to keep you from becoming like the ice itself." The bat extended its imposing wings. "I simply have these leathery wings, and little fur to keep me warm."

"What are you proposing?" asked the wolf.

"I become you, you become me. A merging between wolf and bat. An ability to combine our life forces so we are both better suited to survive this frigid world."

The wolf pondered the bat's proposal. Should he accept it? Or would he perish in the cold of the cave?

Come morning, neither bat nor wolf had left the cave. Instead, a smaller, leathery creature, not quite wolf and not quite bat, emerged, taking in the cool morning air as if breathing for the first time.

\*\*\*

"Whoa, *Abuelo*!" shouted little Emma.

"That's crazy! Is that really how the Chupacabra came to be?" asked Santino.

"What do you think, *niños*?" Grandfather asked with a grin.

"Yes, yes! The Chupacabra, the Chupacabra!" Luciana replied.

"Nah, that can't be," said Roberto. "That's just an old fairy tale."

"No?" asked Grandfather. "Well, tell me this then: what comes but once a year and kills our livestock, draining the blood, while leaving the corpse? What predator is big enough to kill a deer and yet does not need its meat, only its blood?"

And with that the children were silenced. The fire died down and a sudden chill enwrapped them as they took in the Legend of the Chupacabra.

# A GAME OF GHOST

## Middletown Township Police Missing Persons Report: Joanna Briggs Molens, Age 5, last seen October 15, 2008

Police are asking for the community of Belford to help find a missing five-year-old girl named Joanna Briggs Molens. She was last seen on Wednesday, October 15th at Belford Park on Main Street at approximately 11:30 a.m. She was wearing a blue checkered dress with a yellow ribbon around the collar. She has light blonde hair, blue eyes, stands at 3 feet 5 inches tall, and weighs approximately 35 lbs. If you have seen her or know of her whereabouts, please contact the Middletown Township Police Department at 555-421-3255.

\*\*\*

## Excerpt from the Middletown Township Police Department Report on Joanna Briggs Molens, October 15, 2008, 1:33 p.m.

911 dispatch call received from a Cathy Hardy regarding missing child at Belford Park. Officer Nick Castelli and Officer Brenda Beltron arrived at the scene at approximately 11:36 a.m.

OFFICER CASTELLI: I arrived with my partner, Officer Beltron, shortly after the 911 call at 11:36 a.m. Mrs. Trish Molens ran up to the car and shouted, 'My baby's gone, my baby's gone, you have to find my baby!' She took us to the playground where she had last seen her daughter, Joanna Molens, age 5. While I scanned the area,

Officer Beltron questioned Mrs. Trish Molens and an additional two witnesses, Mrs. Catherine Hardy, age 35, and her son, Jason Hardy, age 7. Both saw Joanna Molens in the playground at the top of the slide, but neither recalled seeing her come down. This corroborates the statement given by Mrs. Molens. Officer Beltron and I proceeded out in concentric circles looking for the missing girl. After five minutes of canvassing the area and seeing no signs of the girl or any suspicious vehicles or persons, we proceeded to call for backup to search the surrounding wooded areas.

Further case details to be sent to the office in charge of the investigation, Detective Cassandra Harris in the General Crimes Unit at 555-421-3252.

***

## Journal Entry: Trish Molens, November 1, 2008

Dr. Statton suggested I journal what happened on the day Joanna went missing so that I can stop replaying it over and over in my head. Writing it down isn't going to make it stop. Writing it down isn't going to bring her back. Writing it down only commits her disappearance to history. Writing it down only proves to me that she's gone; as these words stare back at me. I hate writing. She's gone. Fuck you, Dr. Statton.

***

## Journal Entry: Trish Molens, November 4, 2008

Okay, you win. I can't sleep, I can't eat. I might as well try to write it all down. Maybe some good will come out of it. I still hate writing and fuck anyone that reads this.

The day I took Joanna to the park, Wednesday, October 15, was just like any other day. Henry had dropped off Bobby at school on his way to work, leaving Jo and I to ourselves. After breakfast, I put away the dishes and helped Jo pick out her outfit for the day. She loves dresses, and even though it was starting to get cold out, she declared that she'd wear her favorite blue summer dress with the yellow ribbon glued onto the scoop neck. She is a true girly girl, and has been since day one. Dolls, dresses, pink unicorns … she is 100% girl, that daughter of mine. That morning I watched her play dress-up with her dolls and create little dramas for them to act out. They were pretty intricate for a five-year-old—something about a game they would play with each other. After she acted out the latest drama, I brushed her hair. Then she looked at me with those big blue eyes and said, *"Let's go to the park!"* She squealed so loudly Princess started to howl, poor pup.

I told her I had to check a few emails and get a bit of work done, then maybe we could sneak off for a quick tour of the park. I left her alone with her dolls and went to work at the dining room table for a few hours.

Right around 11 a.m., I closed my laptop. Joanna's big beautiful eyes jumped out at me. I was so distracted with work I hadn't realized she'd been sitting there waiting for me to finish.

"Now can we go?" She was so insistent that morning. That was unusual.

"Yes, my dear, grab your coat, put your socks on and I'll grab Princess's leash and meet you by the front door. Last one there is a grumpy bear!"

I grabbed our shoes from the front hall closet and leashed up Princess. Once I had my coat and shoes on, I helped Joanna with her shoes. Her feet are growing so fast, I have to remember to get her a new pair soon. Oh wait. Fuck. Fuck fuck fuck. I hate this.

***

## Journal Entry: Henry Molens, November 5, 2008

The therapist suggested Trish and I create journals to help us "cope" with the fact that our daughter is missing. It feels odd to put that into words: "Our daughter is missing." This was never part of the plan. This was never even a remote nightmare possibility. I never once thought that my daughter wouldn't grow old. I never considered that I wouldn't be walking her down the aisle at her wedding. Parents aren't supposed to outlive their children—it's unnatural. But I'm getting ahead of myself. There's still hope that we'll find her alive despite the fact that the police have no leads, or suspects, or even theories as to what happened to her.

Trish has been inconsolable. She is so angry all the time. I do not have the skillset to know how to comfort her. I've never seen her like this, and frankly it scares the hell out of me. I don't think that my wife will ever be the same—of course she won't—I know she won't. But I don't think she will ever be anything like she was. I think that Trish is gone, vanished like our daughter.

I'm a little less worried about Bobby. He's only eleven. He's young, and he'll bounce back like kids do. I hope Trish pulls it together to remain a mother to Bobby. The boy can't take losing his little sister *and* his mother.

As for myself, I'm buried in my work. I've got end-of-quarter reports due, and a boss who's all too willing to fill any void with younger MBA ass-kissers who aren't yet tied down by families. I can't let them see me slip. Not even now. Not ever.

***

## Journal Entry: Robert "Bobby" Molens, November 10, 2008

I have nightmares all the time. Id wake up screaming and mom would come in and tried to comfort me. She says Im sad about JoJo and this was my way of getting it out. I dont wake up screaming anymore. My nightmares are different now—more real than when Im awake. And theyre always the same. JoJo is playing in the park, then theres blackness, then shes gone. I will never tell Mom and Dad my dreams. Mom always asks me about them and I tell her I dont remember. She cant know. I cant tell her. Its my fault.

\*\*\*

## From the Desk of Dr. Amanda Statton, Ph.D., November 16, 2008

It has been a month since Joanna Molens disappeared. In that time, I have treated the parents separately, with Bobby included in the family sessions. There has been little progress made, and I am recommending that Mrs. Trish Molens continue to see me three times a week, Mr. Henry Molens once per week, with family group sessions with Bobby once every other week. I will reassess again in eight weeks.

The Molens family continue to show significant signs of grief over the loss of their daughter and sister, Joanna, age five. Mrs. Molens is still in the anger stage of grief and shows no signs of moving beyond this phase.

Mr. Molens has been reluctant to express his feelings about his daughter's disappearance, and instead has been focused on his wife's state of unrest. Their son Bobby is withdrawn and lethargic and is displaying signs of post-traumatic stress disorder. He suffers from frequent nightmares, which keep him from getting the rest he needs. Two weeks ago, I prescribed Prazosin 10mg to be taken daily, but he has yet to show any significant change. I will increase the dose to 20mg daily: 10mg in the morning, 10mg in the evening.

Bobby seems almost afraid, like he too might vanish into thin air. I have a feeling there is something more that he is not comfortable sharing, and this inability to express himself mixed with his fear and grief over his sister's disappearance is manifesting itself in his dreams.

I have suggested that the entire family continue their daily journals to help them process their feelings, giving them the freedom to express their deepest emotions with the goal of mitigating the intensity of them.

For now, I have also prescribed Prazosin 20mg as well as Ativan 10mg to Mrs. Molens to help her sleep, and will continue to monitor and adjust their treatments over the coming weeks and months.

***

## Journal Entry: Trish Molens, November 17, 2008

Well, another session with Dr. Statton, and more drugs. Great. I'm already a fucking mess, now I'll be a fucking zombie mess. Whatever, I don't care anymore. I just want to find my baby girl. I just want this all to be over.

***

## Journal Entry: Henry Molens, November 19, 2008

What I don't understand is why the police haven't found anything yet. Not one scrap of clothing, no ransom note, no other witnesses, nothing. They even had both search and rescue and cadaver dogs out, but they lost Joanna's scent at the slide. They couldn't pick up on her anywhere else, not even in the surrounding woods. How can a five-year-old girl go up a children's slide and not come down? I know Trish watches the kids like a hawk whenever we're out in public. How could someone walk up to the playground and snatch her up without anybody seeing anything? And there's no way Trish would have let Jo leave the playground or venture off out of sight. Impossible. What the hell happened to my little girl? Where is she?

I'm going out to search again after work tomorrow. John and Casey will give me a hand searching the playground and the surrounding woods. I have to remember to get extra batteries for the flashlights; the light is fading quicker out there these days.

***

**Journal Entry: Robert "Bobby" Molens November 19, 2008**

I dont like taking the pills from the doctor. They make me feel tired all the time. They dont make my dreams go away, they make me feel like Im trapped in nightmares and I have a hard time waking up.

Last night I dreamt JoJo was looking at me and was really mad and asked, *"Why?"* Then black shapes took her and she disappeard. Im so scared, I dont know what to do. I think Im next.

\*\*\*

**Excerpt from the Joanna Molens Investigation Case# 16-36690**

**Detective Cassandra Harris, General Crimes Unit: November 30, 2008**

After being assigned the Joanna Molens case, I proceeded to re-interview Cathy Hardy and her son Jason Hardy at their residence on 286 Campbell Street, a block from Belford Park. I was joined by my partner, Detective James.

Mrs. Hardy stated that at approximately 11:00 a.m. they left their residence and headed to the park. When they arrived, they saw Joanna and Trish Molens. Mrs. Molens was sitting on the bench opposite the play area. Mrs. Hardy remembered Joanna climbing up and down the jungle gym. She described her as wearing a blue dress with a pink coat and leggings. She said Joanna's hair stood out to her because it was really blonde—almost white—and came down her shoulders.

While her son Jason was swinging, Mrs. Hardy saw Joanna go up towards the top of the slide, then heard Mrs. Molens calling her name, *"Joanna? Joanna?"* Mrs. Molens was standing at the bottom of the slide looking up. The slide is covered, you cannot see a child through it until they reach the bottom. Thinking Joanna might be stuck, Mrs. Hardy offered her assistance but there was no trace of Joanna on, in, or around, the slide. Her son, Jason, confirmed that he saw Joanna enter the slide but did not see her come out the end. After approximately five minutes of searching, Mrs. Hardy then called 911.

Mrs. Hardy also stated that there was an odor she could not place around the slide area. She described it as a chemical smell, like sulfur mixed with something burning.

***

## Journal entry Robert "Bobby" Molens November 30, 2008

Im scared all the time. I wish I never took thos stupid cards from Jackson.

I see JoJo now when Im awake. I see her in the closet, in the backyard, in the shower. Shes around me all the time. Even today at school, when I was in class, I saw her walk into the room from the outside window and stand behind the teacher. I looked around but no one else saw her but me. She has black circles where her eyes are. I dont like seeing her.

***

## From the Desk of Dr Amanda Statton, Ph.D., December 15, 2008

It has been two months since Joanna Molens' disappearance, and the police investigation is still underway. To my knowledge, there have been no substantial leads in the case.

This is now the eighth session with the Molens family, and today was my first session with Bobby without his parents present. He was quiet at first, as he is with the family sessions. Then I saw him eyeing a deck of cards I have in the children's toy box. I asked him if he likes to play cards. Then he started to cry.

After a few minutes, Bobby relayed a story about a new card game he had gotten recently. It had symbols on it and it made him feel good when he played it. He described it as a better game than the others because he could be in charge. He kept saying things like, *I didn't mean for it to happen. I didn't mean to make JoJo go away. It was just a game. It was supposed to be just a game. It wasn't supposed to be real.* When I asked him to elaborate, he started to cry and shake violently. After several unsuccessful attempts of trying to calm him, I decided to end the session a few minutes early. I informed Trish of what transpired and asked her to bring him back the next day but to keep a close eye on him this evening. I also suggested that she attend Bobby's session tomorrow to provide him with emotional support.

***

## Dr. Statton's Office: Transcripts from a Session with Bobby Molens, December 16, 2008

DR. STATTON: Bobby, how are you this morning? Were you able to get a good night's sleep?

MRS. MOLENS: Good morning, Doctor. Bobby, answer Doctor Statton.

BOBBY: Um, no, not really.

DR. STATTON: I'm sorry to hear that. I know you're going through a lot right now. Please take a seat and let's talk. Now yesterday, Bobby, you started to talk to me about a card game you were playing. Can you tell me a little more about that?

BOBBY: It was a game I got from Jackson. It's better than D&D. The cards were cool and felt good in my hands, like tingly. They had these symbols and just one or two colors on them and then the rest of the card is black. There's words on the top that tell you what to do once you roll the dice. I couldn't get anyone to play with me so I played by myself.

DR. STATTON: Is there a name to this card game Bobby?

BOBBY: Jackson didn't know. He got the game from his older brother. I tried to find it online but I only found gamer chat rooms and I'm not allowed in those. The box had some symbols and letters on it that I didn't understand.

DR. STATTON: Mrs. Molens, have you seen these cards? Do you know what Bobby is referring to?

MRS. MOLENS: No, I don't. Bobby, where do you keep these cards? I've never seen you play with them.

BOBBY: I threw them away. I threw them out once JoJo disappeared.

DR. STATTON: And why did you do that Bobby?

BOBBY: (crying) Because they made JoJo disappear!

DR. STATTON: Bobby, you didn't do anything to make JoJo disappear. This was a terrible accident. I'm sure the police will find her soon.

BOBBY: No! You don't understand. I made her disappear. The card game directed me to do it and I did. When I couldn't find anyone to play with, I made

JoJo sit with me. When it was her turn to roll the dice, I picked up the card and it said 'Become a Ghost' and it had a shape on the card, kind of like a square on top of another square and a star right in the center. I hadn't seen that card before, which was weird 'cause I had played it a lot by myself already. I told JoJo that she was now a ghost and she had to act like she was dead. She really didn't understand, but she agreed to lie down and not move. Then she got bored and went to play in her room.

DR. STATTON: When was this, Bobby?

BOBBY: The night before she disappeared! (sobbing) The game did something, made her turn into a ghost! I see her all the time. I can't stop seeing her, but it's not her. It's something bad, but it's not her!

DR. STATTON: Bobby, it's not your fault. Cards can't make people disappear, that's not real.

BOBBY: They are too real! They made Jenny in math class talk to me. They made Mom give me an extra hour of TV before bedtime, they made the bullies in my school go away. They're real!

DR. STATTON: You were bullied in school Bobby?

MRS. MOLENS: He had a terrible problem with two older boys, brothers who kept harassing him. They'd been tormenting him since the previous school year. We went to the principal and the school counselor, but those kids would still find ways to harass Bobby. Then just after the new school year started, the boys were transferred to another school district. Their dad had gotten another job elsewhere. But Bobby, the cards didn't do that, that was just a coincidence.

BOBBY:    No it wasn't! I pulled the card 'Make them Go Away' the night before they left. Every time I pulled a card it came true the next day. I didn't think it was real until JoJo disappeared. The cards made her a ghost. Now I know they're real. That's why I threw them away. (sobbing loudly)

MRS. MOLENS: It's okay, Bobby, I've got you, I've got you.

DR. STATTON:  Let's go ahead and end it there for today. Can you return the same time tomorrow?

MRS. MOLENS: Yes, of course. Come on Bobby, let's go home.

## END OF TRANSCRIPT

\*\*\*

**From the Desk of Dr Amanda Statton, Ph.D., December 16, 2008**

Today's session with Bobby and Trish Molens took an unexpected turn. Bobby confessed to playing a card game which he's convinced is the cause of his sister's disappearance. He was not sure of the name of the game, but said that it had odd symbols on it which he could not decipher. I will ask my assistant to research this before our next session tomorrow.

\*\*\*

## From the Desk of Dr Amanda Statton, Ph.D., December 17, 2008

My assistant was able to identify a few card games that loosely match Bobby's description. She had to dig for hours into gamer chat rooms to find them, as most are no longer in print or for sale in the primary market. The one that stood out was a game called *The Alpha and the Omega*. We couldn't find a manufacturer or a website of origin, only a few chat rooms where they were selling the used decks. There wasn't much chatter or discussion on this particular game, the only description we could find was that it contained Celtic and Egyptian magic. The cards match the description Bobby gave, black except for a symbol and a word or two at the top. I had my assistant order it.

My hope is that if Bobby sees that the cards are harmless then he will let go of the guilt he feels about his sister's disappearance.

\*\*\*

## From the Desk of Dr Amanda Statton, Ph.D., December 23, 2008

The last few sessions with Bobby Molens and his mother have been consistent with Bobby claiming to be the reason for his sister's disappearance. Today, the card game *The Alpha and the Omega* arrived at my office just prior to our session. The symbols seem to be taken from various cultural references: runes, hieroglyphics, sacred geometry, and alchemy. There wasn't much for instructions, save for a small slip of paper instructing the player to roll the multi-sided dice and draw the appropriate card, then the card would direct the game scenarios.

When I showed Bobby the cards, he started to shake uncontrollably. He confirmed this was the game he'd played, and asked that I not bring the cards any closer. I carefully removed the cards from their case and showed Bobby that though they might look a bit scary, they're just cards. Just like we see scary things in a movie or on TV—it's not real, it's just make-believe. To prove my point, I shuffled the cards and rolled the dice. He begged me to stop but I continued and drew the appropriate card which was titled, "Lose your mind." I told him there is nothing here to fear. That we'll resume our session again tomorrow and he'll see that we all have our minds still intact.

\*\*\*

## Middletown Township Police Incident Report: Amanda Statton

## December 24, 2008.

At approximately 3:33 a.m., neighbors called 911 after hearing the sound of a single gunshot coming from the home of Dr. Amanda Statton at 1730 Lynch Road in Middleton Township. Upon arriving at the vicinity, Officer Lingley found no response and proceeded to walk the perimeter of the property. When Officer Lingley came upon the backdoor, he saw that it was ajar. On entry, he found the deceased, Amanda Statton, dead of a single gunshot wound to the head from an apparent suicide. The Smith & Wesson 354 was found in her hand with no other bullets remaining in the chamber. Forensic teams were called in immediately to secure the scene. Officer Lingley canvassed the rest of the area to confirm no other victims or residents were in the home.

### Journal Entry: Henry Molens December 28, 2008

I think Trish is going to have a nervous breakdown and Bobby isn't too far behind. After Dr. Statton's suicide, both of them took a turn for the worse. Trish hasn't been making any sense—talking about some card game and feeling like she's losing her mind. And Bobby keeps to his room and rarely comes out, not even to eat. They both seem to have snapped somehow, and I'm the only one keeping it together.

I tried to provide some normalcy for the both of them. I thought a Christmas tree would cheer everyone up, along with a few presents I had wrapped and placed underneath. Neither of them even noticed. I asked my parents to come over and lend a hand, but not even my mom's patented double-chocolate chip cookies could bring a smile to Bobby's face. I confessed to my mom I was in over my head, and they agreed to come by more often to help out. I don't know what I'm going to do.

At least this diary Dr. Statton recommended gives me some outlet. I have no one else to talk to about this. No one else understands. I'm in danger of losing everything. My entire family is falling apart and I feel helpless to do anything about it. I can't keep holding them up like this. I'm breaking and if I break, who will take care of them?

# JEAN-PIERRE DE ROCHET

The French Loire Valley hosts grand estates which litter the countryside with the rich opulence of noblemen showcasing their wealth and importance. Jean-Pierre de Rochet dreams of occupying one of the many majestic chateaux he visits along his trade route. Traveling past the front entrances, through resplendent gardens towards the stables, Jean-Pierre is reminded of his place. He is not allowed to enter through the front door. He must consign himself to peddling his fur pelts to the servants of the household, never to be greeted by the owners of the estates.

After long days of travel, Jean-Pierre is less than presentable with his suntanned skin, mud-spattered attire and manners unsuitable for the likes of French aristocracy. Even the servants peer down at him, never bothering to meet his gaze. He, a merchant's son, is not worthy of their notice. Jean-Pierre loathes them. In his eyes, the only difference between himself and those that owned the chateaux was birth.

Jean-Pierre often fantasizes that he may, in fact, be French nobility. His first eleven years were spent in the Abbaye Royale de Fontevraud before his father acquired him from the Abbess. He knows nothing of his real father. He could very well be selling fur to him on his route. His adopted mother, Claire Marie, loves him and tells her boy that he is as much a son to her as the two children she gave birth to a decade before. Both children tragically died before the age of ten, making Jean-Pierre the sole heir to his father's business and possessions.

His inheritance consists of a small parcel of land, a three-room farm cottage, one horse, ten pigs, three goats and a dozen chickens, along with a healthy stock of fur from his father's partners in the north.

His adopted father, Phillip de Rochet, taught him the trade and espoused hard work, never ending the day before all business was done. A pleasant, if somewhat modest life, keeps Jean-Pierre well fed and comfortable.

Nevertheless, Jean-Pierre wants more. He craves a life of leisure, of not having to traverse the relentless terrain through every season from bitter snow to festering heat with a horse and carriage both in need of replacement. He wishes to be invited to balls and to eat the finest French cuisine: little cakes with frosted tops, fish pâté decorated in exquisite designs, all served on lavish platters of silver and gold. He desires the freedom to select a wife among the nobleman's daughters, and a mistress, or two, from the servants.

***

One hot August afternoon, while Jean-Pierre daydreams about a life of luxury, he stumbles upon an imposing figure standing in the middle of a crossroads. This mysterious form is cloaked entirely in a gray shroud with a hood that clings to the back of a skull. As the fur trader approaches, he sees a gray, wiry beard hanging down at great length. There are no homes nearby, nor is there any sign of the stranger's horse or carriage. It has taken Jean-Pierre half a day to reach this part of the valley, and he has not encountered anyone until now. His horse neighs at the sight of this being and refuses to venture any closer.

Undeterred by his braying horse, Jean-Pierre calls out to the figure standing in the crossroads. "Good sir! You startled my horse. Are you lost or in need of assistance? I see here you appear to be on your own?"

The elder, for he does appear ancient upon further inspection, raises his head and looks directly into the young man's eyes. An icy breeze runs through Jean-Pierre despite the sweat pouring down the sides of his face. Being of a lower class, the young fur trader's son was not used to people meeting his gaze.

"Jean-Pierre, I am not the one who requires assistance. But, perhaps, I may assist you." The gray form speaks with a voice like timber falling in a distant forest.

"I am sorry, sir," returns Jean-Pierre. "Do I know you or do you know of my late father, Phillip de Rochet?"

"I know all about you, Jean-Pierre de Rochet. Perhaps you should dismount so that we may discuss your desires under the oak tree." The figure gestures with his head to a shaded area under a cluster of oaks.

With an equal mix of perplexity and intrigue, the young man dismounts and walks towards the elder, reins in hand, but his horse protests.

"Fine, stay here in the blazing sun." He lets go of the reins and joins the cloaked figure.

As they take refuge from the sun's rays, Jean-Pierre finds a stump to sit on while the creature in gray remains standing.

"Jean-Pierre de Rochet," the old one begins, "is not your birthright, for your patronage holds a much greater destiny than that of a fur trader's son."

"I knew it!"

"Your true father was well-known across all of France. He traveled in every region and was revered and feared wherever he went. Your mother, however, was of no consequence, and died at your birth." The man speaks as if he is bored with speech itself.

The young man is transfixed. "Sir, how do you know this? Did you know my real father?"

"I more than knew your father. I created him."

"Sir?" He feels dizzy from the afternoon heat.

"Jean-Pierre," the figure continues. "I know in your heart's desire that you, like your father before you, seek power beyond your current station in life."

Jean-Pierre jumps to his feet. "Yes! Yes, I always knew I was meant to be something more than a fur peddler."

The young fur trader stands, looking into the man's eyes, noticing that they are as gray as his beard, as gray as his cloak. It is as if the man is made of smoke itself. There is an orange flicker behind the slate of the man's eyes.

The voice beneath the hood continues. "A half century ago, I met your father at this same crossroads. He, too, sought to become more than what life had handed to him. He wanted to become powerful, wealthy, and to have his pick of the fair maidens. Not unlike yourself, eh, Jean-Pierre? The apple does not fall far from the tree, as they say."

The cloaked figure encircles Jean-Pierre, inspecting him in the process. Their eyes lock together. The fur trader is beginning to feel more unsteady on his feet, and sits down on the stump once more.

"Sir, I do not know if it is this heat or the news that you bring me, but I do not believe that I am well."

A sly grin stretches across the gray man's face. "I have an elixir for you. The same one I offered to your father decades ago. It will cure all ailments; it will strengthen you and make you more powerful than anything you can imagine. Nothing will stand in the way of you and that which you desire."

The gray man produces a tiny teardrop-shaped vial from within his cloak. It has an iridescence to it that glows even under the shadow of the oak trees. The sight of the vessel makes his spine lurch, as if trying to escape the confines of the skin. He feels a wave of heat well up inside him, culminating in a ball of fire between his temples.

"Sir, what is that? It is enflaming my body!" A mixture of excitement and confusion flood his senses.

"This, Jean-Pierre, is the key that unlocks the door to your destiny."

And before the young man's eyes, the figure transforms into a swirling wind of gray dust, spinning into a small cyclone until nothing is left, save for the elixir now in Jean-Pierre's hand.

The vial feels cool to the touch and much heavier than he anticipated. It is like holding the cold steel of a pistol or the handle of a rapier. Without another thought, Jean-Pierre removes the crystal topper and pours the liquid contents down the back of his throat. He swallows. The taste is that of sweet honey and copper. He feels nothing at first. He looks around for signs of the old man, but there are none, only his own horse looking back at him from the crossroads.

As he stands, he notices his dizziness is subsiding. He breathes in the summer air, and it revitalizes his spirit. Looking down, he realizes the vial has disappeared. He searches the grounds, his garments, and the base of the tree. Nothing. The bottle has vanished just like the gray man.

"Humph, maybe it was all a dream due to this blasted sun," he says out loud to no one in particular, save maybe for his horse. "Yes, that must be it, I must have pushed myself too far today." As he walks towards his horse, the memory of the ashen figure fades with each step.

Mounting his horse, the animal begins to protest with several neighs. "What has gotten into you today? I will have none of your nonsense." Jean-Pierre notices how easy it is to lift himself onto his horse; as effortless as taking a breath. He proceeds on his journey with his wares in tow, stopping a few hours later to camp for the night.

With each hour that passes, his memory of the encounter under the oak trees fades into a dream-like haze. He struggles to remember the words spoken—something about his real father, and a liquid. The bittersweet taste of the potion is etched in his memory. But like an opposing magnet, the harder he tries to remember the details the more the memory pushes away.

Jean-Pierre sleeps restlessly. He dreams of a man's face, one not unlike his own, but with darker features, more facial hair about the brow and along the ears, and darkness around the eyes. He wakes to the sound of an animal crying out in the night. He looks up to find his horse still tethered where he left him, and drifts off to sleep once more. The next day, his route takes him to the Chateau de Chenonceau, resting on its majestic stone-arched foundations over the Cher River. Owned by the Duc de Vendome, the chateau is used as a hunting lodge and a place of retreat for the French noble family. The fair maiden, Marguerite, is the youngest daughter of the Duc, and is revered for her untouched beauty, her alabaster skin, her auburn hair.

Approaching the chateau, Jean-Pierre is intercepted by the head house servant and directed to the livery at the back of the main living quarters. As he rounds his horse towards the stables, he catches a glimpse of Marguerite sitting against a window, brushing her lush, auburn hair in the morning light. Her beauty matches that of the chateau, with its flowering gardens, manicured lawns and budding rose bushes kissed with dew.

A heat rises within Jean-Pierre, a mixture of lust and fire. He feels his member enlarge at the mere thought of caressing that beauty, of conquering Marguerite's delicate frame. His body begins to shake, first with a slight tremor, then graduating into a violent seizure. He does not know what is happening to him—and is surprised that he feels no alarm at his sudden reaction. All at once the fire within him gives way to an uncontrollable need—that which he has never felt before. His eyes remain fixated on Marguerite.

A nearby servant rushes over to offer aid, but Jean-Pierre pushes him away with such force the young boy crashes into the back of the stables breaking several bones in the process. It was as effortless as swatting a fly and done with the same amount of consideration. He focuses solely on the object of his desire: Marguerite. He walks, then runs, towards her window, his clothes falling off as he approaches.

The frame of his body transforms. As his inferno rages, tissue and sinew bulge throughout his body. Every muscle flexes into something superior to what it had ever been before. He feels taller, leaner and, as he continues towards the window, he hears the sound of an animal crying out—like the night before, except this time the sound is emanating from his own mouth.

He scales the wall with ease, and within a few leaps is upon the window, staring face-to-face with the young object of his desire. At the sight of him, Marguerite screams and runs back towards the great hallway, leaving Jean-Pierre to peer at his own reflection in the morning sun.

Staring back at him is not the face he was born with. It is not a face he has ever seen before. Looking back at him is a massive, hairy creature with eyes like burnt charcoal outlined with flickering orange flames. Thick, coarse hair sprouts from the face, growing longer the more he stares. Looking down at his hands, he notices that they too are becoming enveloped by the same gray hair: wolf fur. He loses his balance and falls backwards into the courtyard with a hard thump. The fall steals his breath, but only for a moment. He quickly recovers and takes off on all fours into the woods beyond the chateau, desperate to escape the monster's reflection.

Jean-Pierre traverses the forest with ease. He is able to leap great distances and can see, with crystal clarity, the minutest insect from a hundred yards away. After running for over an hour, he eyes a doe with her fawn grazing in a clearing. A fire within him burns with hunger, and without a thought he leaps upon the unsuspecting pair, ravaging first the doe, then the fawn. His first kill. Warm blood pumps from their veins into his. It is euphoric. He lets out a howl, the guttural sound of an animal that has conquered its prey, victorious.

"I see the new skin looks good upon you, Jean-Pierre." A voice from behind him echoes against the trees.

As he turns his head, he sees the cloaked figure standing at the edge of the clearing. Jean-Pierre tries to speak but is only able to push out high and low-pitched cries.

"You no longer possess the vocal cords of men, Jean-Pierre, for you are no longer human. You have transformed, just as a caterpillar blossoms into a butterfly. Ah, but you are magnificent to look at, just as your father was." The gray form moves, reaching within a few feet of the newborn creature. "Do you know that a caterpillar remains a caterpillar for the first quarter of its life before turning into a butterfly? It has reached adulthood before its metamorphosis takes place. Remarkable creatures. Imagine spending a quarter of your life forced to crawl on the cold, damp earth, then taking flight for the remainder—never needing to touch the ground again."

Jean-Pierre sits on his haunches, listening intently, the fire building up inside him.

"You, Jean-Pierre, are like a magnificent butterfly. You are not meant to spend your life contained within a meager human existence. Since your birth, you have been destined for greatness. Just as a butterfly takes flight, you too emerge into your true form, a creature with limitless power and strength. For it is that desire within you, that fire that burns with such force, that gave way to the inner beast." The ancient one looks upon his creation with admiration and awe.

Jean-Pierre, unable to speak, struggles to absorb these words. He is starting to lose his grip on language. He is starting to lose himself.

The gray cloak continues, "Jean-Pierre, you will no longer be the adopted son of a fur trader. No more will you have to work and toil for your most basic sustenance. From this point forward, you will be your true father's son: a man reborn, a wolf. The elixir I gave you merely provided the catalyst to become that which was already inside of you. It was your yearning and your birthright that completed the transfiguration. You will find that more of your human self will die as you give way to the fire of the wolf. You will be able to take all of that which you desire without consequence, without remorse, for you will have left those shackles of your human existence behind."

What once was Jean-Pierre de Rochet now stands tall in the forest, towering over the cloaked man. The gray wolf looks down upon his creator and takes in the scent of his flesh, realizing the figure is long dead. There is not a trace of blood or tissue, only the smell of decay and rot. The stench burns the wolf's eyes, and he shakes his head, retreating into the woods and leaving the gray-cloaked figure behind.

# IMHOTEP

Darkness has been my only companion these last four thousand years. A void of light, sound and sense encompasses me with unrelenting monotony. Trapped in a decaying shell, unable to will my body to obey my commands, I remain motionless. A soul bound to earth, denied passage to the afterlife, never facing the great judgment of Anubis. How many years have I ached for wretched relief? How many moons have risen and fallen over the great city of Heliopolis, while I continue to wither in a sea of black? I have only my thoughts and the memory of a life once lived to keep me company.

\*\*\*

As a child, I was unlike any other. My talents and capabilities far exceeded those of my elders. My dreams were filled with the workings of the earth and stars. The gods, Geb and his twin Nut, acted as my guides. The sweet or acrid scent of the soil aided in predicting whether the harvest would be bountiful or spoiled. The moon and the stars above whispered to me just before the mighty Nile rose beyond its banks. The Sphinx spoke to me of its true origin.

My mother revered me; my father feared me. At the age of eight, the Priests of Ra selected me for instruction within the great temple of Heliopolis. My parents did not protest. The towering temple gates, lined with onyx obelisks covered with the ancient scriptures, sent foreign vibrations throughout my young body. My days and nights were spent devouring the ancient teachings. The stars were easy for me to decipher and I memorized each one's placement within the night sky. The elders allowed me to perform the morning rituals for Ra and eventually, I alone selected his clothing and placed his offerings. I became adept at the herbs and elixirs used in treating the sick and burying the dead. But my true gift blossomed when interpreting the ancient scriptures, in a way my tutors could not.

For years I poured through the text and devoted myself to the teachings of the gods. Their wisdom, which they once bestowed onto man, was lost over time, until I rediscovered it. Unlike my fellow priests, I deciphered the symbols and writings left by Thoth, Osiris, Horus and the mighty Ra. The more I studied, the more I felt their presence.

I uncovered the rituals necessary to commune with the Great Ones. They spoke to me and I listened, and I learned. They showed me the beginning of the universe, when all life began. I was taken to the future when all came to an end. I saw the significance of the tiniest speck of sand and the irrelevance of the cosmos. I spent every waking moment with the divine. They favored me above all others; they made me feel special, and I adored them.

\*\*\*

As the gods took me under their wing, Pharaoh Djoser became jealous. Djoser—who I served and aided—felt threatened by my proximity to the gods. The royal court came to *me* for advice on the harvest; they sought *my* guidance on public affairs, asked *me* to negotiate contracts and marriages. They did not ask their King. I gave good counsel and people trusted me, for my tree always bore fruit. That was my undoing.

One morning as I began preparing for the Lighting of the Fire ritual for Great Ra, I noticed none of my fellow priests met my gaze. Before I lit the fire, Djoser stormed into the room and grabbed the torch from my hand. "Imhotep, you are no longer permitted to perform the daily rites. I have assigned another to take your place." As he spoke, my fellow priest, Anatun, entered the temple and was handed the torch by Djoser.

My heart felt leaden with these words. He ushered me out of the room and motioned for me to follow.

"You are forbidden to give counsel to anyone except me. You are to serve your king alone, and no other." His face was red with anger and I sensed this had been brewing within him for some time. I left his chambers unnerved.

In my quest for knowledge, I lost sight of my place in the world. I forgot who was in charge, and Djoser would *never* let me forget it. And that was my curse: my hubris.

I needed to prove to my king that I was loyal to him. I designed an elaborate monument, one that would tower into the heavens and last for all time. Bathed in the Great Rays of Ra, this pyramid structure would have no equal. Once Djoser saw this masterpiece dedicated to his reign, I would fall back into his good graces.

\*\*\*

Construction began, and I was given a thousand workers to carve and shape the limestone rock in perpetual shifts. I gave them the instruments I forged from sand and instructed them on how to measure and cut the stone so that each block was identical.

Under the moon of Isis, I erected each stone into place using the ancient knowledge of Thoth. Nothing was spared in the creation of Djoser's monument. All resources were given to me to complete it.

\*\*\*

As the structure took shape, Djoser became softer to me, allowing me back into his company. We dined together, and he shared with me his dreams of the future and of his plans for his next life. I shared with him the ancient teachings I studied and described how I trained my mind to hear the gods speak to me. He found this fascinating and asked me to teach him how to do this for himself. We spoke of philosophy, of the stars, of the evolution of humankind. We debated on the news of the day and planned the trade routes along the Nile. Though he was my king, we became friends.

As the pyramid tomb neared its completion, the pharaoh summoned me to his chambers. "I am surrounded by many enemies," Djoser began. "It is rumored that my young nephew Sekhemkhet is threatening to unseat me and take over my reign."

"My king, I know of no such threat. Are you sure?" I was dumbfounded. I knew Sekhemkhet to be an impetuous man-child, but did not think him ambitious or intelligent enough to plan a coup.

"He is greedy and a fool and is easily influenced by those who council him." Djoser took a sip of wine from a golden goblet laced with red garnet at the base. His eyes peered at me over the cup's brim.

"Is it possible to bind a soul to the body upon death?" His voice lowered as he leaned in closer to me. "Are there rituals that can prevent a soul from entering into the afterlife?" Heat radiated from the back of my neck as he spoke. My palms began to sweat.

"Yes," I explained, "there are a few passages in the Book of the Dead that speak on such binding rituals. A priest draws an Anubian inscription on the inside of the sarcophagus, using the blood from the living victim while speaking an incantation. When performed together, the rite would burn the bridge to the afterlife, keeping the soul forever entombed inside the body. But the sacrament must be performed during the winter solstice, when the night is at its peak, before the sun returns." I pondered his request. What actions could warrant being denied the afterlife? I shuddered at the thought.

Djoser looked at the ceiling and nodded. "Bring the passage to me."

\*\*\*

With the autumn harvest coming to an end, the work on the pyramid neared completion. As the light days of Ra shortened, I felt a great apprehension, knowing the winter solstice was approaching. I planned and prepared the ritual for Sekhemkhet as instructed, but felt uneasy about condemning anyone to such a fate. I secretly included a measure to break the curse; one so simple Djoser would not suspect it.

***

On the eve of the winter solstice, my solace was broken by palace guards who ushered me into Djoser's chambers. I demanded they unhand me, and was met with silence. In the center of the torch-lit room stood Djoser, surrounded by every priest in the temple, all eyes were on me.

I will never forget the last words spoken to me: "Imhotep, you served me well. The monument you built for me is a great feat to your genius and ingenuity. For that reason, I shall make this swift. I cannot have you follow me into the afterlife, for there I will be the supreme leader, taking my rightful place alongside the mighty Osiris. I cannot and *will not* have you usurp my power and authority again."

It happened with great speed. I was forced down the lower chamber of the temple, where bodies are prepared for burial. The warmth of the fire did not ease the chill as my clothing was stripped from me. My protests went unanswered. Shoved onto the embalming table, my mouth and eyes were bandaged first, cutting off my air and sight. More hands wrapped my body in soaked cloths. I gasped for breath as the bandages tightened until, one by one, I felt each of my ribs break in succession, puncturing my lungs. The priests chanted the incantations while the knife sliced across my neck. Blood rushed into my throat and ears, and I remember the final thought of my mortal existence: *I will never see the Great Sun of Ra again.*

Then, darkness.

***

I do not know how long it took for my body to die. It hardened around me. Though there was no pain, there was constriction; a tightness that became maddening. I felt trapped in a tomb with walls continuously closing in. I lost all sense of who I was. After a time, there was nothing left of Imhotep. That being died along with the body. All that remained was untamed hysteria.

And darkness.

***

I am unaware as to when I awakened to my present self. When one goes mad, untethered to any sense of reality, something snaps and resets, like a broken bone.

All at once I remembered Djoser's betrayal with renewed hatred. I poured every ounce of myself into the construction of his pyramid, preserving his legacy. How can a man I served my entire life, condemn me to such a fate? Had my transgressions been so egregious that he would imprison me for all time?

No.

If I ever escape this prison, I will erase the name of Djoser from all existence. I will go back to the tomb I created for him. I will summon him down from the gods; I know the spell to bring him back. I will delight in slicing into every inch of his immortal flesh until there is nothing left of him but fragments too minute to fit beneath a fingernail. I will scatter his remains into the four winds, and will command the Hawks of Horus to feed upon what is left. I will then find all of his descendants, and I will end them. I will reap my revenge.

But Djoser was just a man, weak and insecure with his own failings. Of course he deceived me. His ego disallowed anyone to be superior. That superiority could not continue to threaten him in the afterlife. His actions, though extreme, were predictable—as all men are.

No.

The true betrayal was that of the gods who deserted me, they watched as I rotted in my prison. Immediately after my burial they ceased talking to me. They left me here as if I were a piece of trash to be swallowed by the never-ending sand. I dedicated *my life* to them; I worshipped them with all that I was and gave them all that I had. I believed in them. I believed they loved me and cared for me as much as I loved and devoted myself to them. There was nothing more I wished than to be in their presence in the life hereafter. And yet here I remain, alone in the darkness, forgotten, abandoned.

For this neglect, I will unleash the fury I have amassed for thousands of years. In my studies, I learned their secrets. When I communed with them, they told me each other's weaknesses, their hidden truths. I know the true name of Ra. I hold the power to destroy them all. Fire will consume the heavens as the gods fall to Earth. I will entrap them into physical form and bury them alive, leaving them to the sand. And like Djoser, I will erase them from history. And I will do it slowly, so that they will scream for all eternity. They will know what it is like to be betrayed, to be orphaned, to be cast out. They will experience the terror and madness I have endured. I will make them lose themselves and wish they were never created.

I just need someone to lift the lid and the curse will be broken, my secret measure.

Darkness still.

Endless Darkness.

What is that sound? A vibration surrounds my tomb as the earth moves above me. Dirt begins to loosen and fall. I hear voices. There is a pounding near me.

Light.

# Zombies are Real

Zombies are real. No, not the *BRAINS, BRAINS!* type of zombies you see in the movies. Zombies aren't reanimated corpses with various body parts falling off as they drag themselves through suburbia. The zombies I'm talking about are less obvious, and much more terrifying. You wouldn't know a zombie until you looked one straight in the eyes.

My maternal grandmother was a tough woman that came from a world that made her so. She was one of a dozen siblings who moved to San Francisco from Mexico, and whose father abandoned the family when she was young. The older siblings took care of the younger while their mom—my great grandma—did her best to provide for her brood.

One afternoon, Grandma showed me a scar on her arm from when she broke it playing stickball in the Mission streets. Apparently, she was pretty good at the game, and held her own against boys her age. During World War II, she worked in the Richmond shipyards to lend a hand as a real-life Rosie the Riveter. She never let her background, her gender or her ethnicity hold her back. And I looked up to her.

My grandma drove us in her stick-shift through the streets of San Francisco to visit her mother every weekend. Now to those who don't know, that's pretty badass. Some of the streets in the city have an incline well over 30 percent grade, which means you're basically driving straight up into the sky. This is a challenge for even the most seasoned driver; I won't do it to this day. My grandma did it all the time and never batted an eye. She was fearless. Until she changed.

\*\*\*

Grandma could also be terrifying. She was able to whistle through her teeth loud enough to call us in from blocks away, and when she whistled, we knew we'd better come. If one of us disobeyed her in any way, she would not hesitate to spank our backsides until they were as red as the geraniums on her porch.

\*\*\*

Back in the '90s, my brother had a turkey farm up in mountain country, and in his first year he recruited his family to come help with the 'harvest' for Thanksgiving. Living in the city all my life, I prefer to get my meat in sterile, plastic-sealed packages, free from any trace of blood, at the local market. The idea of having to help process a turkey farm was as foreign to me as another language. But he was my brother and he needed help, so I went.

I was nauseated by the idea of slaughtering turkeys. And to make matters worse, my brother had *named* them all. They were his pets throughout the year; they followed him around the property and he knew each one of them, their personalities and special quirks.

He lined them up on the makeshift wooden guillotine my brother-in-law helped to build and regaled us with stories about each turkey before they met their bloody end: "This one here likes to snuggle; this one George, he's my favorite; Judy here likes to be hand-fed her corn …" You get the idea. It was awful. I was horrified, and just wanted it all to end.

The one person who wasn't fazed by any of it was Grandma. She looked at me with disgust and said, "Where do you think your food comes from?" and "What's wrong with you?" When my brother was having a particularly difficult time with one turkey, Grandma walked over (by this point she must have been in her late seventies), grabbed the turkey by its neck, held it over her head, and swung it around as casually as if it were a cowboy's rope. The neck snapped instantly. We all stood back and watched her in awe. She was incredible.

*\*\**

When my mom died of cancer, Grandma was never the same. I kept her company while my grandpa went on his Sunday trips to the flea market. She looked at me and asked, "Where's your mother?" and I'd have to tell her over and over again, "She died, Grandma." Each time it was like she was hearing it for the first time. She cried and yelled and demanded to know why no one told her that her only daughter had died. We were both so devastated by the exchanges that I started to lie to her, "She's fine, out shopping."

There were times when I looked into her eyes and saw a sparkle of the woman she once was, but most of the time I met only a blank stare. She was physically awake, but her brain had checked out.

Grandma started to wander off in the middle of the night. She frequently left the house and shuffled through the darkened neighborhood streets in her slippers and nightgown, directionless. These nighttime excursions were so frequent my uncle had to put an alarm on the front door to prevent her from escaping.

As her disease progressed, her fear intensified. She often woke up at night and, not recognizing her husband of over sixty years, screamed that a stranger was in her bed. He ended up sleeping on the floor in the living room to ease her fears. Everything frightened her: neighbors, delivery men, family members, invisible hallucinations. I was heartbroken to see this independent, strong woman who I admired and looked up to all my life, become a scared child needing to be soothed, placated and distracted from her reality.

Towards the end, in the nursing home, there was no longer a trace of the woman I knew growing up. Her eyes had a glassy sheen to them, like milky marbles, as she stared off at the ceiling. Grandma was alive but she was also dead. And she stayed in that state for years—several long, heartbreaking years.

Grandma was gone, but her body remained. I could no longer find her in those eyes. The true horror was seeing and witnessing someone I loved die before me, and yet her body refused to give up the ghost. My grandmother was a zombie—but not in the way that you think.

# WENDIGO

White. That's all I see. That's all I ever see. White on the trees and white on the pavement and *oh goodie*, more white on my car, which I now have to shovel off in order to go anywhere in this godforsaken place. Fucking snow. How did I let Toni convince me to move out here? I'm a California native. I'm used to coastal fog, sunny days year-round, and the occasional earthquake, never this constant relentless barrage of snow. I hate it. I can't even leave the house half the time. How do generations of people survive here without going postal on each other?

It was pretty at first. Like living in a white winter wonderland theme park, except instead of riding rides you'd slip and fall on your ass in your own driveway. I will never understand why people *choose* to live here. I get that if you've never known anything else you wouldn't know how awful it really is until you leave. But folks that actually pick up from anywhere else and then decide to live here? Madness.

And I guess I fall into that bucket.

One of my many new tasks out here is chopping wood for the fire, which is a steep order since I can barely feel my hands half the time. Toni says I'll get used to it. I doubt it. The axe gets heavier every time I lift it. It's almost as if my muscles are getting weaker, not stronger from the repetitive motion. My biceps start to quiver when I'm only a few logs in. I am really not cut out for this.

And to make matters worse, today there was a terrible smell just past the tree line, behind the tool shed. The odor was so awful— like meat gone bad. An animal must have met its end out there. It is curious though; with this amount of snow you'd think the freeze would hold the smell. Snow hides everything. Toni said it was probably bear scat. Great, so not only do I have to contend with the snow, now there are bears on our property?

"Don't bears hibernate during the winter?" I asked her.

"Some do, some don't. If there's enough food around to sustain them during winter they don't have to hibernate."

Toni knows all things.

***

It's a new day, which means more chopping. My hands are so numb I don't even feel the blisters forming until they pop and ooze into my gloves. That'll be painful once they warm up by the fire.

The smell is back, and it's pungent. There is an odd acrid stench to it, like sour milk, raw meat and vinegar mixed in a food processor. It's nauseating, challenging the contents of my stomach. And there is something else, too—a creepy feeling, as if something is watching me, surrounding me from all sides. Scouring the woods for signs of movement, all there is to see is white.

The woodpile is high enough for now. Toni will be coming home from work soon. I hear tree branches breaking—something moving in the trees behind me, big enough to knock the snow off the cedars. I think it might be—

Wait, Toni's home—I hear her car pulling into the driveway.

***

Tonight, as we were settling in to watch a movie, the power went out. A flighty Nor'easter decided to change direction and came a day earlier than expected. Toni says the power is usually only out for a few hours when this kind of thing happens, and we should be good by morning. She grabbed some extra blankets and a flashlight from the hall closet, and we turned in early.

Well, she was wrong. It is now morning and still no power. It feels as cold in the house as it does outside. How do people stand it? Don't they have extra insulation in houses out here? And I'm so hungry this morning. I must be putting on a layer of winter fat. How does food go bad in the refrigerator when it is still freezing in here? If I knew that the power would be out all night, I would have put the food out in the snow. Oh wait, bears. Scratch that. There's got to be something here I can salvage; my insides are twisting I am so hungry. All that wood chopping must be eating up too many calories.

\*\*\*

There's no work for Toni today. All the roads are completely shut down. Looks like another night of blankets, cold and darkness.

I'm gathering more wood for the fire, as that might be our only source of warmth for the night. God, I have got to find some food. The wind keeps slamming tree branches up against the windows, making all these banging and scratching sounds. It unnerves the senses; the silence broken by nature's violence.

\*\*\*

Settling in around the fireplace, Toni hands me a tepid cup of tea heated by the fire and begins telling me tales passed down from her Algonquin grandmother.

"She'd always tell me to stay indoors when the weather got as bad as it is now. She would talk about a creature that lived in the wilderness and craved human flesh. She called it a 'Wendigo', and explained how this creature was once human, and was weakened by greed, cold and hunger. They were usually outcasts in the community and didn't quite fit in with the others. The spirit of the Wendigo would then possess the person during a moment of weakness, turning them into a Wendigo. Once the transformation took place, they would be forever forced to roam the earth feeding on human flesh."

My stomach began growling.

Toni continued, "Wendigos are soulless creatures with an unquenchable appetite. They have been known to chew their own lips raw and even eat their limbs if no other food source presents itself. In one story, a young boy escaped to a village after being enslaved by a Wendigo. When the tribal leaders went to confront the creature, they chopped off his legs—only to find him sucking on his own bone marrow upon their return.

"The Wendigo often stalks the weakest link in a group: the young, sick or those who have strayed from the community. They hunt their victims like a wolf hunts a deer. Some of their victims they devour, others they turn into Wendigos like them, if they sense that same hunger within them.

"My grandmother told me about a tribal leader who was killed for thinking he was a Wendigo. Apparently, he went mad and killed another family in the tribe, and was found eating their flesh in the woods. They killed him instantly before he could fully turn into a Wendigo."

"How did they do that?" I ask.

"Apparently, there was a whole ritual to it. They had to dismember him and bury his limbs in four different directions, far enough apart so that they couldn't find each other again. It's a cautionary tale like *don't go out into the woods alone or a witch will eat you* kind of thing. If you succumb to the cold and hunger of winter, you might become easy prey for a Wendigo."

"But what do these things look like? Are they still human?"

"No, they change their shape. They have a heart made of ice and become tall and thin and always look emaciated despite the constant feeding. They hide in the treetops and blend in with the snow so that any unsuspecting prey won't see them coming. The only thing that gives them away is their smell. According to my grandmother, they have a horrible smell."

Something prickles on the back of my neck. "Could it have been someone who was schizophrenic or psychotic? I mean people do crazy things during the winter months. Look at the Donner Party."

"I think it was more of a cautionary tale of what not to do when the winters are long and you live in a small community. Don't be greedy and horde everything for yourself when food gets scarce. Putting your own desires above others is what could turn you into a Wendigo." Toni continues, "But you're right, Cassie. Legends always have some kernel of truth. Maybe someone did show signs of psychosis and start eating people; it wouldn't be the first time. Now let's hit the hay, I'm tired. And you don't want to stay up late or the Wendigo will eat you!"

"Haha, very funny."

***

There's something about Toni's tale that is unnerving. No, I don't mean the Wendigo itself; that's just made-up nonsense. But there is something about human nature—that we have the capability to go to such depths as cannibalism, whether for feeding a real hunger or due to breaking with reality. It's unsettling to think about. One minute you're a member of society, the next an outcast— a pariah feeding upon those you hold most dear.

After piling on layers of quilts passed down from each of our grandmothers, we settle into bed and welcome sleep. But nightmares peppered by hunger keep breaking up my rest.

In one of my nightmares, Toni and I are sharing a meal together, holding hands in a French restaurant. We're seated outdoors, the sun is shining down on us, and the Arc de Triomphe stands in the background. Then I look down on the plate and see I am cutting into her hand, slicing into her palm with my steak knife, carving out a piece of the fatty flesh at the mound. I stab my fork into it and place the bloody meat into my mouth while Toni stares at me lovingly with her brown eyes. I wake and sit up straight, plastered in my own sweat despite the cold. Droplets run down my back like icy fingertips.

I get up and walk towards the fridge. I find nothing staring back at me. I check the lights—still no power. From outside, I hear a shriek like the cry of a barn owl, followed by movement in the snow. The crunching sound is undeniable. Something is definitely out there.

The remnants of the dream are still etched in my vision. Toni's loving stare as I cut into her flesh is the most disturbing. It felt as if she wanted me to do it, like she gave herself to me in an act of selfless sacrifice, the ultimate gift. I shake my head, trying to erase the feeling, and find myself doubled over in pain. It feels as if something cold and sharp is clenching my stomach, squeezing and pumping it as if to extract whatever might be left in it.

I fall to my knees. My mouth opens in gasps as I heave bile and bits onto the tiled kitchen floor. The darkness is broken up only by the reflection of the moon on the refrigerator door. My eyes water as I fight for my breath, unable to scream or call out as the convulsions take over. Something skitters across the floor, accompanied by the sound of scratching against the cold tile. I catch a quick flash of a shadowy thing moving from the back porch through the kitchen and towards the bedroom. Towards Toni.

I have to get up, I have to warn her.

Something is wrong. My legs feel different, longer and less stable. I look down through tears to see spider-like legs, gray and thick at the thighs then narrowing down to needle points at the tips. They protrude from my hips, alongside my real legs, which are shrinking back up inside me. There is no pain, only the intense clenching in my stomach. I try to stand on my new legs and find myself falling forward, only to catch myself with the same spindly arms that had grown out of my shoulders. My hands and arms shrink to doll size and are absorbed into my armpits. Only tiny fingertips stick out.

I try to scream, and instead am struck with a shriek so piercing that it reverberates off the walls and back to me in a sonic echo. I try to cover my ears, only to find small holes instead, smooth against a hairless scalp.

Part of me still wants to protect Toni. I have to get to her. I force my new body to move towards the bedroom, I slip and fall on a face no longer my own several times before making it to the threshold of our room.

Toni is sitting up in the darkness, waiting for me. I try to speak but am met with more chirping shrieks—my voice box is completely gone. She holds up a mirror in one hand and the axe I've come to know and hate in the other. I move closer and see myself in the mirror. The horror looking back has a burnt charcoal face with thin, sagging skin, hanging like tiny sacks at the jowls and neck. The eyes—I recognize my eyes—they're the only part of my reflection that is still me. As I stare, they go from hazel to a deep black. And as they change, I feel the axe strike my neck.

# Spreckles

Spreckles paced the workshop with nervous anticipation. Her oversized feet had carved grooves in the wooden floor over the years. She knew the big day was coming, and when he awoke, he would be hungry. Her team still needed four more in order to make their quota. The enormous vats of green and red were only partially filled. She needed them to reach their goal, marked in red candy-cane tape at the top of each container.

Spreckles was her given name, one bestowed on her by her master. She used to be called Samantha, but that was a lifetime ago—a faded memory of a past too painful to recollect. There were only seven more days until Christmas, and the flurry of consumption was nearly at its pinnacle. It was time to harvest the remaining four.

Her team had been up against a tight deadline before, but she'd never been in charge, not until now. This was her first year leading the project and the consequences of failure, well … she put that out of her head. Each year her data analysts would calculate the top six nicest and naughtiest on the list for a total of twelve. The variables in the algorithm calculated the ratios of nice vs. naughty per annum at a rate proportional to the number of years lived. Her team scoured the entire globe, each continent, each city, and town looking for the best and the worst this year had to offer. They left no stone unturned. The final report was originally due two weeks ago, but there had been a glitch in the computing stream; something in Central America was blocking their data collection. When a team went to investigate, they disappeared.

This left Spreckles with two less than desirable options. One: send out another search party to find the missing analysts and retrieve the remaining data stream; two: use the data she had to harvest the remaining four, and hope her boss would not notice there was anything amiss.

But who was she trying to fool? He would know if data was missing, and the outcome for selecting the wrong twelve would be catastrophic. With only seven days left, she needed to complete that list and harvest the remaining four. There really was no other option. She had to go herself.

Spreckles packed her materials and left her subordinate, Winky, in charge, with strict instructions to follow. In her absence, he was to proceed with extracting the final four, assuming the list they had was complete. In the meantime, she headed off in search of the missing data and her team.

***

Spreckles was not used to being back in the world. She had been isolated in the North Pole since before her ears and feet grew. Being in the magical workshop stunted her growth. She remained the size of a young child, except for her ears, nose, and feet. They continued to grow at a normal rate, giving her an elfish appearance; a mixture of youthful innocence and aged wariness. She needed to bring a hat to shield her ears. There wasn't much she could do about her nose and feet. Darker shoes would help her feet blend in with her surroundings, not the bright green slippers she found herself in most of the time.

With her mission planned and her team selected, she set off to the underground sleigh tunnels, a network of connected highways deep beneath the Earth's surface. She set their coordinates for the last known location of the missing team, and they were off, shooting through the center of the earth in a silver-bullet-like-sleigh in darkened tunnels lit up by red and green bulbs.

Her chosen team members were at the top of their game. Pepper was the head of reconnaissance and mapped out the areas where the previous team went missing. She had been with the old man for over a century; she never failed a mission, and her mapping skills were unmatched. She saw into every trap and each opportunity. Jinxy was the youngest of the group. He was less experienced but had a clearer memory of what it was like to be human. He had only turned a decade ago, so his ability to help them blend in with the locals was crucial. And, finally, Cogs was the lead data analyst and knew how to find the glitch in the system. He wrote most of the original algorithm and knew the programming inside and out. If anyone could find the missing data, it was Cogs. And Spreckles' job was to keep them all safe, find the missing team, and bring back the final dataset. They only had twenty-four hours to complete their mission, or there wouldn't be enough time to harvest the remaining four. They had to make every second count.

Spreckles had set up radio comms with Winky back at base. The team was to stay in constant communication while being monitored by their gumball tracking devices. There was nowhere in the world they could not be tracked. Spreckles told herself this, despite the previous team having the same trackers, as she slid through the tunnels, ready to make her exit.

The sleigh shrieked to an abrupt halt, slamming each member against their red ribbon seatbelts. The team disembarked with military precision. They each grabbed their equipment and followed Spreckles out of the tunnel. Jinxy surveyed their clothing, pulling their hats below their ears and tucking extra toes into shoes too small for their feet. The heat was sweltering. A night and day difference from their workshop. It took them a minute to adjust to the humidity in the air and the brightness of the blazing sun. Spreckles cursed to herself, wishing she had thought to come in the darkness instead of under this scorching heat lamp. But time was imperative and even waiting a few hours until nightfall could jeopardize the entire mission. They pressed on.

Cogs took out his monitoring device and found a weak signal from the data stream, due south. They trekked through the dense forest, cutting through brush and warding off insects the size of their heads. Spreckles spotted forest sprites stealing glimpses of them from behind flower buds and tree hollows. There was no time to stop and socialize; they were on a mission. She ignored them and ventured on.

After a few minutes, they came to a clearing in the forest—a wide, expansive square with a grass carpet only about an inch tall. Pepper pulled out her navigation system and determined they were at the ancient Mayan site of Altun Ha in the northeast region of Belize. She advised them to stay within the covering of the trees and avoid stepping into the clearing. They had to evade detection.

As they circled the perimeter, Cog's meter flashed a rapid candy apple red as it pointed towards the great pyramid in the center of the square. They quickly maneuvered through the outer edge of the forest until they were facing the back end of the monolith. The signal was strongest there.

Voices approached, and the group fell back into the covering of the forest. A set of adult tourists with cameras and oversized brimmed hats, all smelling of suntan lotion, started climbing up the back steps of the pyramid. Once the tourists were out of sight, they made their way to the base of the pyramid. Cogs determined that whatever was causing the data glitch was coming from inside the ancient structure.

Pepper scanned the back edge of the pyramid with the terahertz spectrometer and saw movement from within the thick stone walls. She used her thermal scanner to detect temperature fluctuations and found a cold spot at the bottom right corner of the pyramid's base. They noticed a small hole, partially covered by leaves and loose dirt, that looked recently dug. This must be where the previous team had entered. Spreckles ordered Jinxy to shovel around the hole in order for them to gain entry while the rest remained on lookout. A few times they jumped back into the forest while tourists traversed up and down the pyramid's exterior. As Jinxy hit a gush of cool air, Winky radioed back to Spreckles. There was a problem.

Retreating back into the forest, Spreckles learned that their master began to stir, showing signs of consciousness. He was not supposed to wake for another six days—this was highly irregular. She comforted Winky and reassured him that he was just adjusting in his hibernation, to not disturb him in any way and continue on with their mission. He reported back that they recovered two of the four remaining to be harvested and had teams out in the field to collect the two outstanding. They were to report back within the hour.

Spreckles closed her comms and returned to the group. Jinxy unearthed a small opening that emitted a radiant blue glow. Pepper analyzed the light and particle waves and determined they were safe for entry. Spreckles went first, followed by Cogs and Pepper, while Jinxy remained on lookout from behind the tree line. As each of the three squeezed into the hole, they noticed a distinct smell of damp earth mixed with a synthetic substance. Pepper's devices showed high mercury levels—deadly to humans. The human part of these elves had long since been erased.

They turned on their headlamps to find themselves in a vast, undisturbed cavern filled with pieces of gold, pottery, and the sound of running water. It was cool underground, a welcome change from the sweltering heat outside. Cogs analyzed the data disturbance and found a substantial amount of radio and electromagnetic waves coming from an area, thirty feet to their left. As their headlamps illuminated the spot, the trio discovered a spiral stone pathway that led deeper into the cave. Pepper and Cogs looked to Spreckles who nodded, giving the go ahead for them to descend.

As their lamps hit the bottom, they noticed an elaborate stone slab on top of a tomb-like structure, decorated in hieroglyphs with gold overlay and splashes of red dye. Spreckles eyed a long crack down the center of the slab that looked recent given the lack of dust around the edges. Pepper pulled out her language analyzer and scanned it over the ancient writing. After less than a minute, her device flashed orange-yellow, signifying the translation was complete.

Pepper's childlike, elfish voice echoed in the cavern. "This Ancient One preyed upon the people in Altun Ha. It is the

Devourer. Our priests entombed him with a magic to make him sleep forever. Do not disturb this tomb, for if the Devourer reawakens, he will be unstoppable." Pepper and Cogs looked at Spreckles who was losing her patience. They did not have time to waste, and she wasn't interested in an archeological expedition. They had to find that missing data, and her team.

Cogs analyzed the electromagnetic waves of the tomb, concluding this was the source of the data disturbance. Ignoring the warnings, Spreckles used her magical strength to pry apart the crack on the slab, widening it enough to see what was inside. Their headlamps illuminated a rotund figure, still full of flesh and bone, wrapped in a red cloak lined with white fur. The figure's face was rosy red, with cheeks that looked as fresh as the morning dew. The chest rose and fell in a slow melodic rhythm. A slight snore slipped through the slightly opened, scarlet lips.

All three elves looked at each other in horror. This was their master—or a doppelganger. Careful not to wake the creature, Pepper continued to read the writings on the tomb.

"Here lies the great one who sleeps.

He awakes but once a Haab' to feed.

We give of our most precious to …"

The glyphs became illegible. Pepper, Cogs and Spreckles knew this story. They heard it each Christmas Eve before their master awoke. This was another creature—one like him, but not him. Why and how? Too many questions bounced inside their heads like bees, but there was no time to find answers. They had to move.

Cogs determined he could repair the data glitch if the tomb were moved to higher ground. The tomb containing this other-master was throwing off the electromagnetic frequency, causing the data to stop flowing. The three carefully resealed the lid and started the herculean task of exiting with the sarcophagus on their shoulders. It must have weighed a hundred times more than their combined weight. But they were used to carrying heavy loads; the red sacks were full by Christmas Eve. As they made their ascent, none noticed three child-sized skeletons. The team was so engrossed by the discovery of another master, they failed to see the dark corner of the cave that hid the remains of their missing colleagues. A pair of green slippers clung to skeletal feet. The rest of the bodies were nearly dust, fed upon by the entity housed in the tomb.

After far too long they reached the exit and helped Jinxy dig a wider hole for them to extract the stone tomb. Night was beginning to fall, and time was running out.

Spreckles' comms device pinged. It was Winky. His voice sounded even, with a sense of forced control. "We have the remaining four. Should we proceed with the extraction?"

Spreckles paused then consulted with Cogs. "What is the probability that this missing data stream would alter the top naughtiest and nicest?"

Cogs replied, "One in a billion. But remember, if it's wrong, it would be catastrophic. It could mark the end for all of us."

She radioed back to Winky. "Hold on, secure and prep the four for the final stages of harvesting. I'll be back before the last star of the night fades."

After ensuring all the tourists had vacated, the quartet dragged the sarcophagus into the forest, covering the hole and leaving no trace of their visit. Cogs double-checked the equipment, assuring Spreckles there was no longer a trace of the disturbance found around the pyramid; all of his instruments confirmed it was only the stone structure which housed the doppelganger. After trying to reconfigure the data and bypass the electromagnetic frequencies, Cogs realized his field equipment was no match for this problem. They would have to bring the massive stone sarcophagus back to base.

Spreckles was faced with another, less desirable option.

She knew what happened if her master awoke too early from his hibernation. She assumed it would be the same for his double. She pulled out her brown pouch with a snowflake design, reached in and grabbed a pinch of the white dust. She blew this into the crack of the stone slab.

She hoped—no, prayed—that this would keep it locked in slumber until their return.

The moon was high in the sky when they finally reached the tunnel entrance. They called up another sleigh and strapped the stone coffin inside it. They locked the two sleighs together with Cogs, Pepper and Jinxy riding up front and Spreckles riding with the sarcophagus in the back. All the while, Cogs was radioing back to his team at headquarters giving instructions on what he would need ready when they returned.

*\*\**

Night gave way to a new day as Spreckles and her team reached their destination. Looking at her watch, she was reminded that they only had a few short days left to meet their quota. It was going to be tight, and they had to act fast. A dozen elves helped to unload their unwanted cargo, placing it carefully onto a metal handcart with wheels each the size of a child's head. Once during the trip, Spreckles thought she heard a moan coming from the coffin, but she'd dismissed it. This time, however, there was no denying the sound that came from the stone sarcophagus: a low growl.

Spreckles locked eyes with Pepper. They knew what that sound meant. Before either one could utter a word, fat, round fingers emerged, yanking Pepper back into the darkness. There were no cries or screams, just the sound of chewing and crunching. They had to move. Cogs looked back at Spreckles, who wiped a tear from her eye and told him to do what he had to do. She got on her radio and called in the head of security, Dixie. Within seconds a team of bigger elves—those turned near the age of twelve, the upper limit of their kind—came forward with laser wands with glowing orange ends charged with enough power to put down an elephant. Spreckles prayed it would be enough. They fastened an enchanted licorice rope around the coffin, further locking the lid in place.

Once inside his lab, Cogs was in his element—directing his subordinates and analyzing the data on theater-sized screens throughout the room. He had a theory, and he was right. A recent earthquake with a magnitude of 7.3 had hit the Altun Ha area the day the data went missing. It must have cracked open the sarcophagus of the doppelganger, releasing the spell. As this second Santa emerged from its slumber, it had created a vacuum of energy around it, sucking in all electromagnetic, radio and microwaves, preventing the data stream from reaching its final destination. It was as if its presence created a black hole, sucking in energy around it and trapping it within. They had never experienced this before, their Santa slept in a Faraday cage which blocked any such interference. They needed to create a similar barrier for this second creature in order to collect the remaining data stream.

Spreckles gave the go-ahead, and Cogs' team manufactured another cage for the creature while she checked in with Winky. The workshop was alive with elves working on the final stages of the harvest. The green vat housing the Nice Essence was nearly full, with only 16 percent remaining until it reached capacity. The Naughty Essence vat was still 55 percent short. The red sparkles that shone through the glass mocked Spreckles with ironic cheeriness. It haunted her. She knew where those sparkles came from. It was how she got her name; that and her childlike freckles.

Her master's favorite bits to consume were the sparkles. That's where the essence of a child's soul hid, in the sparkle of an eye. Spreckles squeezed her eyes tight as the memory flooded back to her. It was Christmas morning and, being too excited to sleep, she ventured down to catch a glimpse of Santa. She stumbled upon the massive creature in a bright red suit as he was placing a present under the tree.

What came next still haunts her.

As he turned to face her, with enormous, wet eyes and a grin too big for his face, she cried, and Santa ran up to her and licked her tears. He told her that her sparkle tasted better than cookies and milk. She can still remember the feeling of wet sandpaper against her perfect young cheeks. He grabbed her, shoving her into his enormous red sack, and carried her with the other children back up the chimney. She never saw her family again.

Spreckles wiped another tear from her eye. This was no time to get emotional. She had to act fast or the entirety of their mission, their whole reason for existing, would be destroyed. She inspected the remaining four that Winky's teams had gathered. One would be for the Nice vat, and three for the Naughty. The little girl with brown ringlet curls was fast asleep in her glass snow globe as the sleeping powder circled around her in flurries. She looked so innocent inside, sleeping peacefully, oblivious to the world around her. The globe glowed green.

The next globe housed a plump boy with short brown hair and pudgy legs which stuck out of thigh-length shorts. He slept restlessly, tossing and turning from one end of the globe to the next. His globe was a reddish hue. The next harvest was a girl with stringy blonde hair. She was rail thin and clutched a doll with no head. Her sleeping smile frightened Spreckles. Her globe, too, was red. Finally, the last one housed a pair of twins: a young boy and a girl, identical except for their hair length.

"The report listed them as two halves that made up one whole," Winky volunteered. "They are nothing without the other." They slept, cuddled in an embrace that made Spreckles uncomfortable. Their globe was also red.

Next, Spreckles went to inspect the harvesting equipment. She hated this room. It was cold and sterile and reminded her of the hospital where she had her tonsils taken out. The massive needle that dropped down from the ceiling could easily penetrate a skull, using the small hole in its tip to suck up the needed materials. All seemed to be in working order. She checked one of the many clocks in the workshop as it counted down until Christmas. They had a little over five days left.

They had never cut it this close before. As she reflected on their recent discovery, Cogs radioed in.

"I have the data."

Spreckles rushed back to his lab.

"Take a look at this." He showed her the report.

All the color left her face.

"The data is wrong? How can this be?" she asked.

"Out of the four remaining children we harvested, one is *not* in the top twelve, the little girl in the Nice globe—the one with the ringlets. There is another out in the world who is nicer than this one. We need to find the child and bring her in."

Spreckles' heart sank into her stomach.

Spreckles radioed to Winky, "Start the extraction for the three naughty children." And before he could respond, she instructed another team to return the little girl with the brown ringlets to her home, and wipe her memory.

Spreckles gathered a new field team to retrieve the final one for harvest. Cogs' report had the final child located in the remote wilderness of Alaska. Their tunnels only took them so far—they would have to travel the rest of the distance by foot.

Spreckles prepared her second team and packed her materials. Within ten minutes they were off in the tunnels, traveling at light speed towards their final mission. On the short journey, Spreckles had time to return her thoughts to the second Santa. Were there more out there? Did it act the same as her master? Did it, too, need child sacrifices to calm its hunger, to mitigate its thirst? Were they going to have to harvest another set of children for this new beast each year? Spreckles shuddered at the thought. And before any answers came, they arrived.

\*\*\*

The cool mountain air of the Alaskan wilderness was a refreshing change from the sweltering heat of the Central American jungle. They exited the tunnel, and her navigations lead, Lolly, pointed them in the direction of a mountain peak a hundred yards away. Each member checked their gear and loaded their packs on their stunted backs. They replaced their workshop slippers with more rugged climbing boots, and each had the standard issue wide brimmed hats to conceal their all-telling ears. Being in such a remote location, they had little chance of encountering a human. Still, Spreckles did not want to take any chances. They would stay off the main roads and trek mainly through the wilderness. Lolly had directed the team to a deer path along a stream that had its origin at the mountain peak. They followed it up to their target. They climbed with ease over the slippery rocks, as they were no different from the ice blocks at the pole. One of the first things they learned as elves was how to gain their footing when no footing seemed possible.

Teeny, the team's wilderness specialist, periodically scanned the forest through the trees searching for any sign of life using his thermal heat imaging camera. So far, they only encountered a few squirrels and a mole, until a sound made them all stop dead in their tracks. It was a high-pitched cry, not from a bird or any animal in Teeny's database. This was something foreign, something unnatural. As they moved again, they were met with a huge crash—the sound of a log, twice the size of one of them, landing twenty feet in front of their path.

Spreckles raised her right hand into a fist, giving the stop command, and all were silent. Teeny once again scanned the woods and detected a thermal heat signature coming from a tree behind Lolly. They remained frozen as the heat signature came into clearer focus. A shape started to form ... an enormous beast seven to eight feet tall, walking on two legs, not four. The smell hit them. It was a rotting, putrid smell that reminded Spreckles of the leftovers post-extraction. Lolly dry heaved and Spreckles motioned her to stop. Lolly closed her eyes and swallowed hard, tears forming out of her closed eyes.

Teeny pulled up his database and showed Spreckles a picture on his screen that indicated the creature was similar to the abominable snowman from their home. It must have adapted to this environment, for instead of the white fur to blend in with the snow, in this green and brown wilderness, the creature was the color of tree bark. Spreckles nodded.

She knew what to do. On occasion, they had run-ins with these creatures at the North Pole.

Spreckles motioned silently for Teeny and Lolly to jettison their packs, move into the stream, and hide amongst the rocks. She reached into her side pouch and pulled out a pair of snowflake-patterned mittens with army grade Kevlar and no-slip-grip at the palms and fingertips. She removed her hat and put on a pair of thermal vision goggles. She made sure her hunting knife was still firmly secured to the back of her waist band.

If there had been any other witnesses, they would have been in awe of Spreckles. She moved with grace and ease up branches like a tree frog, finding purchase wherever she landed. She did not make a sound. Through her goggles, she saw the creature one tree away. It moved towards her, and in one swift motion she cartwheeled over one treetop and onto another, landing directly behind the creature. Within a breath, she was on the beast, straddling its gigantic neck with her tiny legs, her mittens puncturing the creature's eyes. Wet goo dripped down her forearms. Each time the creature reached for her, she cut it with her hunting knife until its arms were a sea of red. The minute it dropped its hands, Spreckles brought her knife to its throat and, with her elfish strength, sliced through the creature's neck, opening it to the bone. The creature dropped dead, but not before Spreckles leapt onto a higher tree branch and surveyed her handy work. The beast was no match for her cunning and speed. If she could handle Santa, she could handle Sasquatch.

Returning to her team, Spreckles washed her equipment in the stream. The smell of the beast on her clothes lingered; she hoped that would not compromise their mission. They regrouped and continued on with Lolly and Teeny having a greater respect for their team leader.

The signal to their final harvest pointed them towards a clearing three miles out. They remained in silence for the rest of their journey, each lost in their own thoughts. Spreckles' mind wandered back to the second Santa. She saw only a quick glimpse from her headlamp in the cave. It looked like her master, but slightly different. The facial features were the same: round rosy cheeks, small round nose, white beard, lips too wide, mouth too big. This one seemed slightly bigger around the chest and forehead, and the skin tone was not the alabaster white she had grown to fear, it was more of a mahogany chestnut, like the preferred wood of their workshop.

Spreckles thought he smelled different, too. Maybe it was because she was sensitive to the beast's smell on her clothes at present, but there was something different about the second Santa's smell. It was a sweet honey smell mixed with something sour like spoiled milk. Her thoughts were once again interrupted by comms from headquarters.

"The red vat is now full and has reached its candy cane goal marker," Winky's voice radioed, sounding less even than before. "What is your status with the final extraction?"

"We're a few hours from completing our mission. We'll be home soon," she replied. Before Spreckles could ask about the status of the second Santa, Winky hung up, leaving her with dead air on the receiving end.

With the short winter days, the sun had already begun to make its descent. They were used to short days and perpetual nights at the North Pole. Alaska felt like home. Out of place within the thick wilderness rose a small community of houses nestled together, separated only by a small stream that meandered through the village. Spreckles saw lights on, and instructed her team to wait for her orders. Lolly zeroed in on two houses. They needed to get closer to make sure they chose the right one. Spreckles could not afford to make another mistake.

There was some interference affecting their readings. Spreckles looked up in the sky to see the green and yellow glow of the aurora borealis. The electromagnetic field meter was off the charts, causing their equipment to malfunction. They needed to get their final extraction back to the workshop before Santa woke. She radioed back to headquarters and asked to be patched through to Cogs.

Cogs was ready for her call. "I have the entire network of children mapped out on my computer screen. The target is a girl named Eleana McClintock." He sent Spreckles a high-resolution photo that showed beautiful blue eyes. There was something familiar about the face staring back at her on the screen— something about the eyes. Cogs gave them the exact GPS coordinates, free from any electromagnetic interference. The satellite image he sent pointed towards the small cottage on the left— the one with its lights on.

The team moved into position. Teeny scanned the home with his thermal imaging camera and determined there were three adults and two children living in the cottage. This would make it hard for them to go in undetected. Normally they would make the extraction at nightfall while everyone in the house was asleep, but they did not have the luxury of time to wait. They had to act now.

With a red-and-white-striped rope hanging on his shoulder, Teeny climbed up the gutter to the roof and tied it around the chimney; something he had done hundreds of times before. He dropped the rope down and Lolly ascended. The two elves on the roof would travel down the chimney while Spreckles disabled the family from under the house. Lolly and Teeny were to wait for Spreckles' signal before they started their descent.

Spreckles walked around the perimeter only to come face to face with a Malamute. His snout rose in a snarl, and a low growl emanated from his chest. Spreckles chided herself for not checking for animals first. She was so anxious to get to her target she'd forgotten her basic training: survey the perimeter, secure the surroundings, then proceed with extraction. She carefully reached into her snowflake pouch and pulled out the white powder she had come to rely on more than once on this mission. She placed a thumb-sized amount on her palm and blew the substance into the dog's face. It sneezed, then charged her—only to fall dead asleep before his teeth reached her face. Spreckles surveyed the rest of the property. All was secure. She found a grate that led to the underside of the house. She quickly pried it open with her tools and crawled inside. Spreckles maneuvered under the house by crawling on her hands and knees. Her headlamp revealed frozen spiderwebs that looked like snowflakes caught in time. She turned off her headlamp to locate a light source from above. In the far-right corner of the house a thin beam of light hit the dirt. She crawled closer and peered up into the house. There was movement, and she heard a few voices from her left. She waited and observed. She counted three adults but only one child. She was not sure if the child she heard was her target. She could not get a visual.

She pushed the green button on her comms, indicating to Teeny and Lolly that it was time to move. Through the small crack in the floor, Spreckles inserted a straw-like device that was only a few inches long, and hooked it up to her snowflake pouch. She turned on the device and a flurry of white powder flooded the room. She waited until she heard one drop, then another, until finally all four were on the ground.

Spreckles' comms crackled in her ear. "We're in." It was Teeny's voice.

"Do you have a visual on the target?" Spreckles asked.

"Negative," Teeny responded.

Spreckles crawled back out of the house and went in through the now unlocked front door to find Teeny and Lolly waiting for her, each holding a little hand. The girl staring back at her was their target: Eleana McClintock. Spreckles thought she was staring into a mirror. Eleana looked exactly like Spreckles, save for the aged years. What kind of cruel trick was this?

"Hello, Great Aunt Samantha."

The voice startled Spreckles as much as the words being spoken.

Eleana continued, "I have been waiting for you. I knew you would be coming. I saw it in my dreams."

The girl was not yet nine but had a poise and maturity that far exceeded her years. She let go of Teeny and Lollys' hands, and ran up to Spreckles.

"Come in, we have much to discuss."

Teeny and Lolly looked towards Spreckles for direction, and she nodded for them to follow, giving them little reassurance. The three joined Eleana in the main room and sat on a soft leather sofa in front of the fireplace. Eleana did not seem at all surprised or scared by their presence, or by the fact that her family was now incapacitated, lying unconscious at her feet.

She continued, "I am not like others, Aunt Samantha. I see and know things before they happen. I saw you coming in a dream over a month ago and have been waiting for you every night since. I know what happened to you and what you plan to do to me. I have one question for you before you take me. Why?"

Spreckles was startled by this. Spreckles' mind was racing, but she could not give in to her emotions. She was still on a mission.

"We do what we do to save children. We find the necessary amount of sacrifices needed to satiate Santa Claus. Before our efforts, he would roam the earth untethered, feeding on children as he delivered their presents. The presents were an elaborate ruse used to get him into homes.

"By harvesting the top twelve naughty and nice children, we discovered we can provide enough sustenance to quench his thirst. With one feast a year, we can mitigate the carnage, until the next Christmas. We are the only ones keeping Santa from devouring every child in the world. What we do is horrific—but if we do not complete our task, then the outcome will be cataclysmic."

Eleana listened calmly and nodded her understanding. "And this year, you found a second Santa."

"Yes," said Spreckles, who was still fighting tears, looking back at a reminder of her human life lost. "We do not yet know what this means. I cannot fathom the idea of managing another Santa. He already murdered one of my colleagues, and I suspect he's to blame for several members of my team who have gone missing. I'm afraid of what I'll find when I return."

"Very well, I am ready." Eleana grabbed her coat and put on her winter boots by the door. She gave her family one last glance, holding back tears.

Spreckles opened the door and they ventured out into the dark.

The group made better time at night trekking through the wilderness. The air was cool, and they harnessed a winter flurry, riding it like a wave over the deer path towards the tunnels. Within a few short hours, they were whizzing back through the red and green-lit passageways, heading towards base. Midnight came and went.

They had three days left.

Spreckles observed how calm Eleana was; it unnerved her. They'd never transported a conscious child before. She thought about using her snowflake powder on her, but stopped herself, not knowing why. Maybe it was because she was a distant relative. Maybe it was because she sensed herself in the child.

They arrived through the gumdrop gates and rushed to the workshop. Winky was there waiting for her and stopped dead in his tracks when he saw the last harvest walking towards him. He had never seen one of the children awake before. Well, except for that one time a naughty child choked on a lollipop, but that was only for a brief second, and they'd extracted him immediately afterwards.

Eleana's eyes grew wide, taking in the brightness and color of the workshop. There were toys and giant stuffed animals and workbenches filled with all kinds of tools and equipment. At the back of the room a row of oversized snow globes sat empty with alternating green and red lights. Spreckles remembered what it was like the first time she saw the workshop, nearly seven decades ago. She was so excited to be at the North Pole, in Santa's Workshop. It was every child's dream. But hers quickly turned into a nightmare. She learned what they made in the workshop—and it wasn't just toys.

Winky went to place Eleana in one of the globes, but Spreckles stopped him. She had an idea. She ordered her team and all the elves in the workshop to disperse and radioed in Cogs. She confided to him her plan and he agreed it might work. At this point they had little to lose; the time to act was now. Spreckles switched clothes with Eleana, placed a green cap over her head to hide her normal-sized ears, and hid part of her face with her hair. Spreckles found a knitted cap to cover her own elfish ears and placed herself in the snow globe. Now they really were identical, save for the crow's feet around Spreckles' aged eyes.

Cogs took Eleana back to his lab, referring to her as Spreckles. Cogs ordered Winky to begin the harvest while he and Eleana went to the sarcophagus of the second Santa. All of the elves were now busy preparing for the final extraction and did not notice when Eleana-dressed-as-Spreckles helped Cogs wheel the stone coffin into their master's sleeping quarters.

Much like the workshop, the room they entered was brightly colored with wood-cut ceilings decorated with carvings of teddy bears and dolls. It was like entering a fairy tale, on a massive scale. Everything was too big, like walking into a giant's lair. The desk and chair were as large as hills that would require climbing ropes to ascend. A massive wooden carousel hung from the ceiling and circled to the tune of 'Here Comes Santa Claus'. The wooden children riding the carousel horses were crying. Eleana saw this minute detail, and nearly screamed. She felt the terror that lay in this room, the terror every child feels when they go to sleep at night. She was horrified to realize this fear came from a beloved icon, a beacon of hope and generosity. Santa was the boogeyman in every child's nightmare.

And he stirred. Noise came from the center of the room. Below the hanging carousel was an imposing glass cage covered with a thin wire mesh. The structure was held together with wood, and the snow flurries inside blew against the glass. Lying on his side, snoring like the Harley Davidson Eleana's dad owned, was the Santa seen on the Coca-Cola ads … except different. He was much bigger than a human man, larger than any bear Eleana had seen in the Alaskan wilderness. His back was towards her. And then he moved. Perhaps because of her presence, and being so close to his feeding time—he woke. He rolled over to reveal a rosy set of cheeks, a beard as white as snow, and a mouth that formed a wide, unnatural grin as he laid his eyes upon Eleana. Santa was not fooled by a change of clothes. Santa could smell the blood still pumping through the child's veins. And he was hungry.

Cogs quickly stepped between the two and pushed off the stone lid holding the second Santa in his coffin. Now that Santa, too, had stirred—awakened by the smell of a meal within his grasp. Spreckles' plan was working. As both Santas rose to devour their prey, they locked eyes with each other. Recognition first crossed their faces as each met the other's stare—then they looked at Eleana, then back at each other. Spreckles knew her master was not the type to share. They both stumbled out of their cages towards Eleana but Cogs was too fast for them. He pushed the girl through the exit and slammed the door shut, sealing himself in.

While pretending to be her great niece, Spreckles pulled out her snowflake pouch and dusted her colleagues. She could not risk them raising the alarm as she executed her plan. She raced to the lair and arrived in time to see Eleana pushed out of Santa's room. Her brave niece collapsed into her arms, having witnessed the two child-eating Santas. Spreckles had used her own flesh and blood as bait. And she prayed it worked. Horrific screams came from inside the door. It was Cogs. As she fumbled for her key, Spreckles heard a loud thump as something hit the door, then silence.

"No!" she screamed.

Her trusted ally, her right hand, her confidant and friend all these years, had sacrificed himself to save her niece. Spreckles found her golden key, opened the door and entered, closing and locking it behind her.

She was alone and face-to-face with two Santas, now awake, confused and hungry.

They screeched then lunged at her. She retrieved her candy cane grappling hook from her waist and shot it around one of the horses on the rotating carousel. With her incredible speed and strength, she pulled herself up to safety before either of them could lay a round finger on her. She looked down and held up her hand to silence them.

"Hear me now. I have the ability to satiate your hunger, as the harvest is ready. But there is only enough to feed *one* of you. Which one shall it be?"

The Santas looked at each other, then—within the blink of an eye—they locked in battle, sharp teeth gnashing and cutting into flesh and bone, clawing like ravenous dogs. Spreckles surveyed her handiwork. The elves would never be strong enough to kill Santa on their own—but another Santa meant it might be possible for the two to kill each other, or at least weaken them both to the point where they could be killed. Spreckles was counting on both creatures having the same insatiable desire to feed; a desire surpassed only by their greed. She watched as blood and puffs of white hair flew into the air. Alternating cries and growls emanated from the fury. The darker Santa lowered his head and bit into the other's belly, opening a gash, revealing red and green slime glistening with sparkles, oozing out onto the floor. The original Santa let out a scream. He bent down and bit into the back of the other Santa's neck, just as it was gorging on the contents of his belly. Both fell. Spreckles watched as they collapsed onto each other, gurgling and whistling from each of their mortal wounds. It was done. It was over.

***

## Epilogue

Spreckles returned to being called Samantha, though few were left to address her by that name. Some of her colleagues whom she incapacitated earlier with her snowflake dust inhaled a bit too much, for they never woke. The elves took to the sleeping agent a bit differently than humans. The recently turned elves went back to whatever family they had left, and those too old to have family remaining, went off into the world to start anew.

None of them knew how long they would live, especially now without the magic of Santa to sustain them. Samantha suspected she would begin aging at the normal rate, which meant there was little time left. Once the last elf departed from the workshop, she took it upon herself to turn on the gas and light a match. The glow from the tunnel entrance was beautiful; the orange and yellow hues mixed with the pristine white of the snow. Samantha told herself she would never live in snow again.

And as for her brave and intuitive great niece, Eleana, her memory of the North Pole was erased and she was placed carefully back in her home with her loving family, their memories cleared, too.

Samantha thought again about the second Santa, and asked herself if there could be more out there. She shuddered, thinking, *that's someone else's problem now.* Her job was done. It was her time to rest, and try to put the horrors of her past behind her.

# THE GATHERING

On the longest night of the year, when the moon is at its peak and the cool crisp chill of winter whips through the dead trees, ghouls and goblins gather for their annual meeting. None of them can remember when they first gathered, or whose idea it was. For as long as the seasons existed, they find their way back to this small hollow at the edge of the world where all things began.

\*\*\*

An orange wisp of smoke stirred amongst the blackened leaves and from it fire erupted. The glow from the ember hues provided enough light to illuminate each of the attendees now gathered around it in a circle.

"I call to order the Annui Temporis Obscuri Foederis," a booming voice called out into the dark. It was a female voice with a timbre that could make a heart vibrate within its casing. Rustling and murmurs blended in with the night's silence.

"Welcome all, both new and old. We gather to bear witness to each other's tales over the past sidereal year. Some of you may know me by the names given to me by those I have preyed upon: Penanggalan, Shtriga, Lamia, Lilith. You, my brethren, may call me Noctis, for I am of the night that bred me. Brother Noclea, will you take roll call, then read the minutes from our last meeting?"

A gray mass that rippled as it moved like Jell-O freed from its mold, slid forward into the circle.

"All present for the meeting of the Annui Temporis Obscuri Foederis say 'Aye'." Each word vibrated as if hitting a metal tin.

A collective "Aye" from one hundred fifty separate voices could be heard.

"The Ayes are noted." From its gelatinous body the glob pulled out a clipboard and pencil and noted the responses.

"The notes from our last meeting of the collective are as follows: one hundred and fifty-two were present. A motion to move the meeting to All Hallows Eve was put forth, voted upon and rejected. Sister Medusa provided the refreshments and organized the charity raffle for Brother Nosferatu's fang repair, and there was a total of nine entries for the story contest. The third-place winner for the best tale told was that of Brother Apis, for his story *It Could Have Happened to Any of You*. Second place winner was Sister Lamia for her story, entitled *What I Wouldn't Give to Taste Her Again* and the grand prize winner was Loogaroo for their magnificent tale, *One Night, One Club, Thirty Victims*." A light applause followed as accolades were once again showered upon last year's winner, who graciously bowed low in response. With his job completed, Brother Noclea—who was not quite gas, not quite solid—slid back into his spot in the circle.

Noctis stood and spoke again. "Let me remind you of the rules. You may each present a story if you wish, but it must be completed by the time the sand has finished running through the hourglass. Failure to do so will be cause for instant elimination, and the storyteller will be disqualified from telling future tales in the next five meetings. And they will receive ten lashes from yours truly." Noctis stroked a black leather whip in her hands. "Winners will be voted on and announced once the moon has begun to fall. The third-place winner will receive this tasty hedgehog, which Brother Coyote captured before our meeting." She bowed her head towards Coyote. She continued, "The second-place winner will dine on this delicious doe and her two fawns, which our esteemed Brother Leeds donated for our event." Again, another acknowledgement, another bow. "And, finally, the grand prize winner will receive the accolades of your peers, a mention in our upcoming *To Hell and Back* newsletter, this stylish midnight cloak fashioned by our one and only Sister Neith, and the feast *de resistance* —the human morsel captured by yours truly."

Applause erupted, followed by what might be considered whoops and cheers. Amidst the applause, a substantial wooden cage was wheeled into the gathering for all to see, the dim firelight casting shadows onto its occupant. A man, half-naked from the waist down, cowered in the cage. A freshly minted gash ran diagonal across his face. One of his eyes was swollen, his lip was bleeding. He was young and muscular and could not have been more than five and twenty. As his eyes met those in the circle, he let out a guttural scream and proceeded to soil himself. The group laughed and howled at his distress, excited for their chance to consume his fear.

"Now," Noctis continued with a look of pride and authority, "who would like to start us off?"

A red-faced demon with horns like a ram stepped forward. His head was far too big for his body, which was petite and stood only three feet off the ground. He cleared his throat and began. "Greetings, fellow Shadows of the Night. I am called Clarion. My tale this evening is titled, *The Girl I Regret Possessing*." The firelight caught the black lines that ran throughout his face, revealing his wrinkled countenance and withered age. Noctis flipped the hourglass.

"It was during the sweltering summer month of August when the opportunity presented itself for me to spoil a young innocent by the name of Rachel. This pale thing with hair like golden strands was not more than ten years old. I wanted her instantly; a desire I would soon regret.

"Rachel came to my attention when she and a group of her classmates gathered around a spirit board. I do love playing with those. They said the proper invocations, beckoning those from the other side to join them. They never specify *which* side—as if there are only two planes of existence: the living and the dead. Humans are so stupid."

A roaring laughter from the crowd erupted in the night sky.

"So naturally, I took that as an invitation, as I had nothing pressing at the moment, having already met my quota for the month. Through the spirit board, I told them I was a young boy named 'Joseph' and I was twelve years old. Little girls want nothing more than to fall in love with another human boy. It's disgusting really"—more chuckles from the crowd—"and they are oh-so-easy to manipulate.

"I learned that Rachel was the daughter of a minister who forbade her from talking to the dead, and who threatened all manner of fire and brimstone if he ever caught her using a spirit board. So naturally, she had to see what all the fuss was about. I should have seen that as a red flag, but I was too far in to pull out now. I told her I had been run over in a horse and buggy accident at the turn of the century, and my greatest regret was never being able to fall in love whilst I was alive. She was putty in my hands.

"Rachel snuck spirit board sessions under her sheets at night. She was a precocious thing, and I couldn't wait to get inside her. She smelled of honey and rainbows."

Jeers echoed from the crowd.

"Don't laugh at me, it's true. She was magnificent. Trust me, you'd want her, too. Now where was I? Oh yes, the nightly sessions became longer and more intense. I quickly learned about her abusive father and her mother who was too meek to utter a word in her defense and of her older brother, Jake, who would steal then break her toys and dolls. I heard her whisper sweet nothings to a boy named Joseph, who didn't exist. I lapped it up.

"Finally, the time came for me to *do the deed* as it were. I told her she could bring me to life if she said this incantation three times, 'I invite you in, body, mind and soul.' Without hesitation this little girl spoke the words with such reverence and eagerness it brought a tear to my scorched eye. Then a quick *pop!* and I was in, looking through her eyes, moving her hands as if they were my own. I don't need to tell you all, but having that beating heart again can be a bit unnerving. You get used to it, though. I surveyed her bedroom as I adjusted to the body I now inhabited. I tried out my new vocal cords and found a deeper octave that was less ten-year-old girl and more forty-something woman with a bad smoking habit. I took a few steps then stopped. I couldn't move any further. This was unusual. When I get full possession, I get *full* possession. Not being able to move the body at my command was alarming. I tried again. Nothing. I spoke out loud in a voice that was threatening, 'Move *now!*' Still nothing. Then from within the skull I inhabited, I heard a chuckle; quiet at first, then deafening. The little bitch was laughing at me! Can you believe it? Me! Clarion, Master of the Dark, Possessor of Souls of the Young and Innocent. Satan's Right Hand— well, *Left* Hand—Servant of the Corrupted. I was incensed.

"Then I heard a voice I'll never forget. 'Who's trapped now, Clarion?' How did she even know my name? Shit shit shit. With the knowledge of my true name, she could control me. I was fucked. There was no way she could have seen through my disguise. But alas. I had been fooled by a ten-year-old girl.

"She continued, 'I could smell your hellfire when you first made contact. You should really do something about that. You reek.' Intolerable little flesh bag. 'Now, I have a few jobs I need you to do.' And she proceeded to tell me of her plot. How a ten-year-old girl, born from a minister, no less, could think up such evil would have inspired envy amongst my demonic brethren.

"First came her brother Jake. The little snot was no use to me, as he was already halfway claimed by the fire pits of Hades. Rachel made me possess all of the toys and dolls he'd mangled so they would first scare the literal shit out of him then, second, torture him as they had been tortured. Her one-eye-remaining Sally Cries and Poops doll got right up to Jake's face and pulled down her drawers and shit real turds in his mouth. It would have been hysterical if I wasn't so humiliated, performing for a ten-year-old. All manner of hell broke loose in this poor kid's room. I got everything that had an on switch turn on and start flashing lights, and moved anything with wheels. Then she made me take his remote-controlled car, his favorite possession—no pun intended— and drive it up his leg to his dick. From there I hit the gas and the brakes on the little machine, and the wheels burned rubber over his blue balls, right through his jeans and shorts, cutting into his young man sacks. This kid screamed all manner of pain, pleading for it to stop, and yet Rachel stood there with me, looking at him, and smiled. Blood escaped from his crotch as he desperately tried to free himself from the car's rubber grip. Smoke mixed with blood filled the air. Ah, the acrid smell of fear and torture. Am I right?" Clarion looked around to see heads nodding in approval as he savored the scent memory.

"Then he dropped, and that was the end of it. His spirit left his body and went through us, calling Rachel all manner of names as he left. I saw him again later when I finally escaped, but that's a story for another time.

"Next was Rachel's mother. She was sitting on her bed catatonic-like despite the screams of torture coming from her son's room. It was as if she was patiently waiting her turn, like she knew what was coming. I never did get her name. Rachel was quicker with this one. A simple choke around the neck and it was over. Little ten-year-old hands found their perch, and with my added strength it took no time to end the woman. She didn't struggle or say a word. It was eerie, even for me. We crossed her arms and closed her eyes. All that was left was dear old Dad.

"Now by this point I learned a bit more about Rachel's dad. He was a fire and brimstone preacher, but not in the way you'd think. He worshipped my boss: Satan Morningstar, Lucifer. This was the first I'd known about it, as we were walking to meet him at his place of work, which was right across the street. Apparently, that's how Rachel learned how to trap a demon; her father's textbooks laid out all the instructions for her.

"Rachel previously shared with me how her dad defiled her in all manner of ways. He must have been drawn to that same rainbow aroma that lured me in when I first laid eyes on her. Not only did the bastard rape his own daughter multiple times, he offered her up to other members of the congregation for their own pleasure.

"When we got down to the basement level of the church, we stumbled onto a ritual of some sort. As I looked around, I wondered what Halloween store they'd raided to decorate their dark lair; it was laughable. There were stuffed ravens, and plastic skulls lit from the glow of red and black candles which dripped wax onto the floor. In each corner of the room, a pair of medieval torches casted light and shadow against the black-painted walls. There were maybe twelve participants standing at the edges of an encircled pentagram, chanting some nonsense that they totally got wrong. Humans are impossibly ignorant. And standing high at a black-stained podium, looming over the others, was Rachel's dad. This guy was something to behold. He wore a red satin robe with a hood hiding his eyes as he bellowed out phrases for his followers to repeat.

"Rachel walked us into the center of the pentagram, and had me speak in my demon voice, as low and as loud as I could make it.

"'Hear me now, children of Lucifer. You have done the bidding of the Dark Master well. He is pleased, and now it is time for you to join Him.' Before they had a chance to react, I extinguished all the flames and locked the only exit, preventing any attempt to escape. I took the torches off the walls, and with the blunt end sodomized each member until the blood that ran from them matched the color of their stupid satin robes. Some squealed in delight, some moaned with pain. Rachel laughed. Gradually the voices quieted down as each soul left their body, leaving only two with beating hearts.

"For her father, Rachel had saved up something special. Again, if I wasn't so humiliated by this girl, I'd be impressed. First, we stripped off that terrible Aleister Crowley knock-off he was wearing, and of course the asshole was naked underneath, sweat glistening down to his limp dick. He had a pot belly on him that would rival a pig, and he smelled as bad. Flashes of his sweaty, fat body on top of Rachel flooded her memory, and it actually made me nauseous to relive it through her eyes. Rachel took back control as she walked towards her father. I was now in the passenger seat waiting for my next set of instructions. She gave him a lecture about the Devil, how He doesn't come for those with trivial and superficial desires. The Devil seeks those with a heart as black as His; a heart willing to torture the good out of every soul. She explained that as he and the congregation repeatedly raped her in His name, He—being Satan, my boss—came. Through their spilled seed, He flew into her—and she welcomed Him in. And once He entered her, He found a kindred spirit. Rachel fantasized all manner of tortures to those who defiled her. She wanted them to feel the same powerlessness she'd felt. Rachel wanted to bring hell upon them, since they had no idea what hell really was. I'll never forget her words, 'Men are small, petty. They think it's all about satiating their little willies and quenching their ever-growing thirsts. You have no idea what it means to be a shepherd of Satan. Let me show you now.'

"And with that, this little girl used my name to call forward a half dozen of my brethren through the pentagram on the floor. Each demon was assigned a body part: one took an arm, another a leg, two others on the opposite side did the same, the final two were assigned the head, the last to Daddy's dick. They penetrated each orifice with their flaming barbed tongues, causing the great minister to shriek like a young child. His eyes, nose, ears and anus bled steady streams of red. My demon brothers then punctured his skin with tiny needles in their fingertips until every pore in the man's body bled droplets of crimson. They worked him into a frothy rhythm, in and out, in and out, as Rachel commanded. Her father's eyes grew wider with fear, fear he had never known in his life until now. Fear that Rachel knew all too well.

"She walked over to him and picked up a knife from the altar. While the demons continued to work on him, she slit the head of his penis into quarters, just at the tip. Then with my strength behind her, we peeled back his dick like a flower with four petals. Ah, the screams that came out of that man ... you would win awards in Hell for screams like that. And this all came from a little girl with blonde golden hair, not more than ten years old.

"After far too long, his screams stopped, and all that was left was a low gurgle. The demons continued with their work until all movement ceased. Then his shadow self emerged from his body, and the demons locked onto him, holding him in their grasp as his flesh body fell to the ground. They continued to torture his soul, poking and prodding it as they had been, and together they slipped back down into the pentagram, back through the gates of hell.

"Now all that was left was me and the girl. I marveled at her. You have to admit, that's some pretty impressive shit she pulled off, even with my help. She then spoke to me. 'Clarion, I needed your strength and your ability to accomplish my task. Satan gave me the incantations and told me how to trick you into doing my bidding. That plus a little help from my dad's books and you were easy to lure. With my task done, I release you now. You may be free to corrupt further innocents. My work here has just begun.'

"And with that, Rachel spoke the words to release me, and I was back in my current form which you see before you now. I have to admit, that was one for the books. I am ashamed that I was hoodwinked by a little girl and do regret possessing her … but wow, what a ride it was."

Clarion bowed to great applause. Some in the crowd criticized him for being manipulated by a little girl and his response was, "Hey, you weren't there. You would have been, too."

Just then the last few grains of sand hit the hourglass, and Noctis spoke once more. "Thank you, Clarion for that delightful story. This Rachel sounds like an impressive creature indeed. Now, who would like to go next?"

A massive green-yellowish figure with a bulbous nose and a body to match stepped into the center of the circle. Each step he took sent vibrations through the crowd.

\*\*\*

"My name is Schlont and I reside, as most ogres do, in a cave in a forest, away from mankind." His voice was like the sound of two boulders sliding against each other. "The story I have to share is titled, *The Hiker, His Dog and a Canteen*. In the spring months I lose my privacy, as hikers venture deeper into the woods after the winter thaw. Once, centuries would pass where I never saw a man or beast, given the remoteness of my location. Now it seems each spring they impede into my domain a little further. I want nothing to do with them. I've had my fun, as I'm sure we all have; popping out of the trees and scaring the living shit out of unsuspecting humans. But that got old after the first few hundred years, and now in my golden age all I want is to live peacefully, alone, with nature and my thoughts.

"So when I heard the sound of whistling near my cave, I grabbed my club and went to inspect the latest intruder. Mind you, I have traps and barricades set up to block any entrance into the cave, though over the years they've become harder to maintain. My strength is not what it used to be, and there have been breaks in my defenses that have gone unattended.

"The view out of my cave is breathtaking. It sits high in the mountain range and overlooks the entire valley below. It gives me a good vantage point, and I can see anything within five hundred miles. The whistling I heard came from the east, and as I sniffed the air I picked up on a male, about thirty-five, clean-shaven, freshly showered, with the day's sweat already upon him. I smelled his virility and knew he was in his prime. I also smelled a dog, a German shepherd, walking alongside the man. They were about two hundred yards from my cave entrance and getting closer.

I headed down the mountain towards them. Typically, when a human gets close, I will throw a large rock in their direction to scare them off, or muster up a low growl that sends them running on their heels. This day was no different. I grabbed a small boulder, took aim and threw it in their direction. I got pretty close, within ten feet of the two of them, just off to their left. But to my surprise, the man did not flinch. The dog jumped and howled, but the man just paused, looked in the direction of the boulder, then looked up in my direction and kept on hiking up towards the cave. I blend in, given my color, so it was not possible for him to see me through the thick forest. So I got a bit closer and summoned my deepest, loudest growl. The new leaves shook and some fell, losing their grip with their mother stem. Still nothing. I wondered if he was deaf. His dog reacted with a terrible yelp, but refused to leave his master's side.

"The man looked up in my direction, and met my eyes. Impossible—there was no way a human sees that well in the forest, especially with the late morning sun casting shadows across the thick brush. Humans barely see ten feet in front of them when they are driving those death machines on wheels. How they survived this long is a mystery to me. They are the most ill-adapted creatures on earth. They cannot even survive a winter's night with their furless bodies, and yet here they are traipsing through *my* forest, near *my* cave. Unfathomable. Whoever created *us* certainly did *not* create humans. They are something altogether foreign to this earth, they are not *natural*."

Schlont received several nods of agreement and a few 'hear hears' amongst the listeners.

"But I digress. This man was now locked onto my location and was heading towards me. I have not had to kill a human in eons. I knew I still could—I was at least three times his size—but still, I steadied my feet and gripped my club tighter. One swift blow, then a drop off the cliff, and no one would be the wiser. He would be just another hiker who tripped and fell off the mountain ledge, and I could go back to my peace and quiet.

"As he got closer, I sensed something different about this man. No matter, he would soon be worm food; I put the strangeness out of my mind.

"A voice that I could not hear with my ears spoke to me: 'I am not here to cause harm.' It startled me. This voice was as clear as anything, and it was in my head. The hair on my back stood on end, alerting me to danger. Who was this human? He spoke to me again: 'My name is Richard and I would like to speak with you.' He was still several yards away, and I lost sight of him on the mountain.

"Before I could gather my thoughts, he was standing in front of me with his dog in tow. He was impressive by human standards. He stood six feet two inches and had deep mahogany skin and thick black hair with long, muscular arms. His eyes were different. His eyes did not match the rest of his dark complexion. His eyes were the lightest blue you ever seen. As if the sky were trapped in his eyes. They were magnificent.

"He spoke to me now, audibly. 'I do not mean to disturb your peace or cause you any distress. I have come here looking for you. I would like to speak with you.' And with that he opened his backpack and pulled out a red metal container, a series of books, and a mechanical device. A package wrapped in white paper fell out, and I knew instantly by the smell that it was freshly cut meat.

"He handed me the package. 'I would like to offer you a gift. It's fresh deer meat, from a hunter who killed a stag not ten miles from here yesterday. Please accept this gift, with my gratitude.'

"I was speechless. I had not the need to speak out loud in several years. Our gathering here is the only time I ever speak, and sometimes not even then. I have never in my six hundred and fifty-five years of existence had a conversation with a human. I never gave them the opportunity to get close enough to communicate. I was stunned by not only his lack of fear, but also how he climbed up the mountain before I could sense him.

"I know I am getting older, but my senses are still keen. I am ashamed to admit that he frightened me, the same way humans are afraid of spiders. Humans are a hundred times bigger than a spider, and yet, the spider strikes a nerve of fear in them. It is irrational. That's how I felt about this man standing in front of me, offering me fresh deer meat. I took the package and kept my club held tightly in my other hand.

"'Why are you here disturbing my peace? How did you find me and what do you want of me?' I asked.

"'I do not wish to disturb your solitude. For that I am truly sorry. I thought you might like some company after being isolated all these years. You see, I've been watching you since I was a child.'

He paused, then looked away, past me in the distance. 'Have you ever heard of *remote viewing?*' he asked. I shook my head no.

"'Remote viewing' he continued, 'is a way for us humans to leave our bodies behind and have our spirits travel to places anywhere in the world. Some of us are born with this gift and some are trained to use it for military purposes. My father was one of those recruited by our government to remote view into foreign adversaries. He was able to go into a meditative state, allowing his consciousness to leave his body and travel to a specific location, anywhere in the world. He could describe military bases with precise accuracy, right down to the number of buildings and what was stored in them. It took him years of training to develop this skill and as you can imagine, he was quite an asset to our country.'

"I had never heard of such a thing. Have any of you?" Schlont looked into the crowd, and most heads shook. One or two nodded in the affirmative. "Well, this was news to me. I thought they could only leave their meat bodies once, and that was during death.

"I responded, 'No, I have never heard of such a thing.' At this point I was still debating whether or not to strike him dead where he stood. But I was intrigued, and his eyes drew me in further.

"'My father trained me to remote view as a young boy. He would go on trips for work and we would play a version of hide and seek. He would be halfway across the globe, and I was supposed to describe where he was and what he was doing. It was great fun, and I was pretty good at it. It wasn't until I was an adult that I realized no one else had this ability. It got so easy for me that I frequently traveled anywhere in the world while never leaving my bedroom. That's how I found you.'

"He continued, 'I have always loved this part of the world for its remoteness and pristine natural beauty. I visited here often and took in the majestic mountains, the plentiful foliage and wildlife. We live on an incredible planet. Out of all the places I've seen, the pyramids in Egypt, both North and South Poles, the Amazon rainforest, the depths of the Pacific Ocean, this part of the world is my favorite. On one of my many visits here I spotted you coming out of your cave. I never saw the likes of your kind before in the entire world, and I was intrigued. I was fearful at first, but then I watched how you lovingly cared for your home and how you blended with nature. You are as natural as the trees, the wildlife and the mountain that we're on. I admired you and I came and visited you often. I thought to myself, *There's another creature that appreciates this part of the world, like me.* I wanted to see this beautiful country with my physical senses and meet another creature that appreciated it as much as I did. May I hear your story?'

"Can you imagine a human coming into your lair with such a tale? Your sanctuary, your base, the only place of peace you have? We've already been pushed into the furthest shadows of existence, and now they dare to encroach even into that space—our home? I felt violated that this man was spying on me with his incorporeal self. It unnerved me, and I was angry and gripped my club harder.

"I told him, 'How dare you violate my home and my privacy? I don't snoop around where you live and watch you unbeknownst. How would you feel if I showed up in your bedroom, unannounced, and said I've been watching you for years?'

"'Huh, I see your point. I never thought of it like that.' Richard looked a bit uncomfortable as he realized how much bigger I was, as I was now standing tall, looking down upon him.

"'Believe me, that was never my intention, I only happened upon you by accident.' He tried to recover.

"'But then you kept coming back, kept watching me. Who is the real monster here?' I was shouting then. I felt the anger within me build up and the ground beneath me begin to shake. I continued, 'What makes you think I want to share my mountain with you? My life, my stories; how dare you? You humans only think of yourselves, never other creatures. I came here for solitude, for peace and quiet. I am not here to entertain the curious and nosy. You have ten seconds to get off my mountain before my club meets your head. And if you *ever* come back in whatever form to spy on me, I'll have your liver for breakfast. For I now have your scent, and when an ogre gets a scent, he has it for life. I can find you no matter what part of the world you run to, and I don't need to leave my body to do it. I will come and you will suffer.'"

With this, loud applause erupted from the shadowy crowd.

Schlont continued, "By now I had almost forgotten about the dog. It was still standing beside its master, terrified of me, yet still he stayed. I was struck by the loyalty of this creature, ignoring his own nature and instinct to run in order to remain with this imbecile of a man. It was curious. It was even more curious that the man simply stared at me without moving, without retreating down the mountain as I demanded.

"This creature had some nerve. As I lifted my club, Richard pulled out a red circular canteen. The kind they store water in. He calmly unscrewed the cap and handed it to me and said, 'I offer you one last peace offering. I researched and studied your kind in the ancient literature and found a reference to a drink called *potio auream,* the golden elixir.' I had not heard that phrase spoken in over five hundred years. It is a drink my mother made to strengthen and fortify our kind. It provided enough sustenance for us to last a century without having to eat a morsel. It is deadly to humans, and extremely difficult to make.

"I sniffed the contents and a flood of memories came swirling back to me. I could pick out each ingredient. He had made it perfectly.

"'How do you know of this?' I asked him.

"'I studied your heart,' he said. 'It's another gift that I have. I can see into any being's desires, and I felt a yearning in you, to reconnect with your past.'

"This was true. I had been contemplating my family, long dead these last several hundred years. I am the only one of my kind that remains.

"'Please, forgive my intrusion; I see it was short-sighted on my part. Accept this gift with my apologies, and I will be off.' The man called Richard turned and headed back down the path with his German shepherd following.

"'Wait.' I was stunned to hear the word leave my mouth. 'Sit. I will converse with you, but then you must go, and never return.' I do not know what possessed me. Maybe it was the *potio auream*— the taste was as I remembered it—or maybe he reminded me of my solitude and it brought a sense of loss to my heart. I cannot tell you why I decided to share my story with him, but I did. I talked of the great beginning when giants roamed the earth; of how the deities created nature and all its inhabitants—save humans. He shared with me his life as a child growing up moving from military base to military base; the constant threats his family was under given his father's occupation, and how last year his father suffered a heart attack and died under suspicious circumstances. I told him of my family, my long dead and beloved mother, Shalant, and my sister Kryna and brothers Gothy and Vornio and how I was the last of my kind. We talked about nature, philosophy and the world as it was. We talked until the sun went down and came up again. It was … nice.

"When it was time for him to depart, he looked up at me with those sky-blue eyes and said, 'Schlont, thank you for allowing me to stay and converse with you. I know it is against your nature to share space with humans and I was wrong to impede upon your solitude. I am sorry for that, but I really enjoyed our conversation. Be well.' And with that, he and his dog stood and headed back down my mountain. For a moment I thought, *What if he alerts others to my lair? I should end him now before he's out of sight.* But I didn't, I let him and his dog leave. I am ashamed to admit it, but I too enjoyed the company, even if it was from a human."

Schlont, having now finished his tale, took a seat back in the outer circle; a few hands clapped.

Noctis spoke, "Come on now, we can do better than that," Noctis clapped more vigorously, encouraging others to do the same. "Let us show Schlont our appreciation for his story. We all know what isolation can feel like. Thank you for sharing, Schlont, and well done. Who's next?" Noctis surveyed the crowd. The sound of the fire breaking through the wood was the only noise that penetrated the night's silence. After a lengthy pause which made some attendees squirm and shift in their respective seats, a voice emerged, followed by movement and shuffling from the far end of the circle.

"Ahem." A smoky white mist came into the firelight and out of the vapor a face emerged and spoke. "I am not sure I am allowed to be here. You see, I was once human." Gasps and grumbles could be heard.

"Is that allowed?" a voice shouted towards Noctis, followed by further inquisitive comments, none of which were in the speaker's favor.

Noctis, taking a hold of the situation replied, "Not all of us emerged from the dark; some of us chose this path. All of us present have a right to be here. You would not have received an invitation otherwise." She turned to the ghost-like figure. "You are welcome here, please continue," she said, and restarted the hourglass.

"Thank you, ma'am. My name is Matthew and my tale is short." There was only a face in the mist, no other discernible shape emerged.

"I lived about a hundred years ago in what is now considered the Wild West of America. I was a cowboy and good with a gun, and I took my share of pain and caused it in kind. I was never particularly philosophical or religious. Living was hard and I figured a dirt nap had to be better than this godforsaken life. So when my heart met that bullet, I welcomed the escape. My life wasn't particularly noteworthy, neither was my death. What came after I died is where my story begins, in a tale I'll call, *My Death Took a Detour*.

\*\*\*

"Once the initial pain and shock of death left my body, I felt myself float up like a balloon, separated from my corpse. I looked down on it and thought, *What a sad and pathetic life*. Then another realization hit me, one that all us humans experience when we die, *it ain't over yet.* Though I no longer had a body, I was still alive in some sense. I wasn't sure if I should be elated or disappointed.

"What came next defied all of my beliefs up until that point. All of a sudden, I was whisked up into this metal object shaped like a fat cigar, except it was silver inside and out. I thought, *Is this Heaven? And if so, I think they got the wrong guy.* But no, there were no pearly gates or angels with wings or a god with a white beard. There were these tiny gray things with huge black eyes. I was in a freakin' spaceship, if you can believe it! Back then I didn't know what the hell it was, but now in hindsight I have more clarity about it.

"These little creatures showed me around their ship and there weren't nothin' but more metallic objects like machinery with knobs and screens and stuff all over. Then they took me to a wide room with floor-to-ceiling windows, and I looked out and saw the Earth below us. God, if I still had a body I would have cried, she was so beautiful. That blue, it was the purdiest color I ever did lay my eyes upon.

"I was flummoxed, as you can imagine, and I looked around and asked what the heck they were and what I was doing there. Then from out of nowhere, a taller one of 'em came out and spoke to me with their mind and said, 'Matthew, fear not. We mean you no harm. You have something that we need, something that we will pay you for.'

"*Pay me for? And for what?* I thought. Why would I need payment for anything—wasn't that the point of death, stuff like that becomes irrelevant?

"The being spoke again. 'You have not quite passed through the veil of death. You are in the in-between. We intercepted you, as we have use for you.'

"'Use for me?' I said. 'You gotta be kiddin'. *I* got no use for me, what could you possibly need from me in this state? I mean, I can't hold a gun any longer, I can't eat or shit or screw, what good am I to anyone or any*thing* for that matter?'

"'We want what you hold in your memory. In your consciousness, you have the key to a problem we have yet to solve.' The creature paused for a spell, then continued, 'How can you love and kill at the same time? The two seem incompatible to us and yet your kind does it quite well. You, Matthew, killed without remorse and yet you still had love in your heart. Can you explain this to us?'

"I was pretty floored by this. I mean, sure, I've buried a few that had it comin' and never thought twice about it. It was survival. *Shoot first or die* was my motto. So I explained that where I lived, you killed or you were killed. It was as simple as that. Sure, some folks got off on the killin', but not me. I saw it as a necessary evil to keep me breathing above ground another day.

"They nodded at me as if I was spewing some great words of wisdom. It was eerie to watch 'em. My momma always told me that the eyes are the windows to the soul, and, well, these creatures, they had none, 'cuz their eyes were as black as charcoal—blacker even. I felt myself shiver, despite not having a body, as I looked into them dark pools.

"'And as for the love part', I told them, 'the only love I had in my heart was for my own dearly departed mother. I was hoping to see her once I finally died. Fancy you guys showin' up instead. My mother was a saint.

"She sacrificed everything for my brother and me to come out west and to try and make a go of it. She did things no woman should have to do to support her sons. You see, my daddy got shot in one of them Indian wars. I never knew him. My brother remembered him a bit, but I have no memory of him. So it was just my ma and my brother and me tryin' to survive in an unforgiving world. I carried a piece of her everywhere I went. She made me a necklace with a piece of her hair inside. I loved her, and was heartbroken when the cancer took her. My brother and I parted ways then, and I had been on my own when I met my end.'

"More of these creatures now had gathered to hear my tale. They seemed to be enthralled by my life, as if it was some great Greek tragedy or something. I didn't know if that's what they were looking for, but that was all I had to give. Then the tall one spoke again. "'Thank you, Matthew. That was truly enlightening. As you spoke, we all felt your love for your mother and it moved us. We now have a better understanding of your kind. We shall release you, so that you may continue on your journey.'

"And before I could utter another thought I was back on Earth, hovering over my body. They had said they intercepted me or something on my way through a veil of some kind, so I waited for whatever the next part of the process would be. I waited, and I waited and I'm still waitin'. I don't know if what they did prevented me from going to meet my ma on the other side or what, but I can't seem to figure out what it is I'm supposed to do. And I never did get that payment they were talkin' about—whatever that was.

"I have wandered this great planet for over a hundred and fifty years and seen all kinds of exotic things, including how technology has taken off in the last fifty or so years, and wondered if the space guys had anything to do with it. 'Cuz the stuff I see now in people's pockets looks like the things I saw on that ship. O'er the years I seen more of 'em too, the spaceships, in all different sizes and shapes. But I never did encounter those beings again. I'm hoping to get some answers, 'cuz, I'm lost. That's kind of why I'm here tonight, to hopefully find someone who can help me understand it all.

"I guess that's it then. I'm done. Thank y'all for listenin'."

Silence again permeated the night sky. All eyes were fixed on Matthew, including a set of deep black pools. Noctis whispered to a creature on her right. Its indigo eyes peered out from behind a hooded cloak. The being then left the circle and disappeared into the night.

"Thank you, Matthew, for your story. It is an odd and sad tale indeed. After our night's festivities, we will see if we can find someone to help you." Noctis surveyed the crowd. "Now, who's next?"

The fire was burning brightly as the stars lit up the night sky. An owl called out in the distance, all else was silent. A tiny creature, less than a meter tall, moved on top of a log in the center of the circle. She had a tan, aged complexion and a pair of generous white feet.

In a deep voice that sounded like the crunching of leaves she spoke. "My name is Ixikili and my story is called, *Be Careful What You Wish For.*"

*\*\*\**

"I come from one of the few remaining places left on the planet that has pure magic: the rainforest. It is a place where Mother Earth breathes life into being; where creation is made and where all life began. Every day, humans bring in their imposing and deafening equipment to bulldoze our home, destroying everything in their path. With every tree, plant and animal they decimate, a part of the forest's magic dies.

"Much like my distant cousins in the Northern Isle," Ixikili nodded towards an elfin creature with bright orange hair wearing a miniature green hat; he was the same size as she but with a lighter complexion and young features, "our duty is to take care of Mother Earth and expel all those who threaten to destroy her.

"Centuries ago, we lived alongside the humans. Their ancient peoples understood nature and treated us with respect, for they understood we were—and still are—the caretakers of the rainforest. They would leave us offerings as a token of their appreciation for maintaining the magic of the sacred place. All that changed when the Light Skinned ones came. They wiped out the ancient peoples, and the old ways and traditions were lost with them. What followed was an era of conquest and greed which continues to this day."

Grumbles of agreement rippled through the crowd.

"We are in a life and death struggle for survival. There are so few of my kind left, we are fighting a losing battle. We have taken to extreme measures to rid our forest of the human pestilence.

"In years past, we would draw humans deep into the forest and show them the beauty and wonder of nature. We performed magic and unveiled parts of the forest previously hidden to them. It was our way of waking them up to our world. We hoped that by showing a few humans the splendor of the rainforest, they would develop a deeper respect for it and would learn to live in balance with Mother Earth again.

"We were naïve, and we failed. The humans only brought stories back of little people luring them into the woods to make them get lost or to cause mischief. They completely missed the point. Over the centuries we evolved our tactics. We became more aggressive. Instead of showing beauty and magic, we unveiled the darker side: the death and decay that are also a part of the natural world.

"Towards the end of last spring, my kind were cultivating the blossoms, preparing for the summer solstice, when we heard a group of people nearby. We have protective charms surrounding our home that make us invisible to outsiders, so we continued with our work—until one of them spotted us. Only a handful of humans have been able to see through our shields; these humans possess a gift of sight rare in most of their population. One of their group, a female with strands of hair knotted up like tree bark, looked in our direction and met my gaze. She had on brightly colored clothes and smelled of Cedarwood and sweat. She spoke to the members of her group and alerted them to our presence. As they came to join her, they looked but did not see us. The female became frustrated, and as she argued with them, we slipped off and vanished into the forest. That should have been the end of it—but a few moons later she returned, alone this time.

"Having her find us the first time was a fluke. The second time was unnatural. The area we inhabit is remote, several hundred miles from any type of civilization and surrounded by thick Strangler Fig, Huimba and Ironwood trees. Their leaves and vines create a canopy of protection too thick for large animals to navigate through, including humans.

"Plus, we've seeded the vines with stinging nettles which, when touched, dig into the skin and cause excruciating pain for the unlucky trespasser. The fact that she was able to find us again was not only alarming, but unimaginable.

"Being one of the elders of my group, I stepped forward to see what she wanted. She spoke to me in a language I had not heard before, but still I understood her meaning. She wanted our magic. She wanted to learn how to control, take and manipulate the magic we have spent centuries cultivating. Did she want to use this knowledge to help her kind? Cure diseases or provide a deeper understanding of the Earth? No. Like all humans, their small petty minds only think of themselves. She wanted to gain power over others.

"I was incensed by her request, and so were the rest of my kin. She brought offerings of fruit and flowers to appease us, as if we could be bribed into doing her bidding. For this brazen hubris and insult, we knew what to do. I accepted her gifts on behalf of my tribe and led her to the stream behind our home. A handful of my brethren followed, waiting for my command. The only way for humans to navigate our area is through the stream. As I mentioned before, the forest is too thick to navigate. We went in silence, floating down the water while she walked unsteadily, slipping from time to time on the rocky bottom.

"After a time, we came upon our destination, the Great Cave. The mouth of the cave stands taller than the great Banyan tree, and is three times as wide. It is so deep that the sun cannot reach the back of the entrance. A look of awe came over the woman's face as she took in the majesty of it. This is a place of pure magic. A place where dreams become reality and reality becomes dreams. It is a shifting place, where time and space do not remain solid.

"The stream that led us to the cave continued through its winding caverns. The water becomes deeper here and is ice cold, despite the heat. My folk have the ability to manipulate matter in this place of magic. Within a minute, we created a floating boat out of a fallen leaf, substantial enough for all of us to fit, including the human. I sat at the front of the boat while my kin were at the back with the woman between us.

"We did not speak except through gestures, and yet I knew the woman felt the energy of the cave. We floated through the entrance into the first cavern, where crystal deposits formed from the bottom and top, meeting together like jagged teeth. The woman's eyes strained to see in the darkness, so I pulled a crystal from the shore and whispered to it until it shone like a star in the night sky. My brethren did the same until the cavern was fully illuminated. The woman spoke with reverence and excitement once her eyes beheld what was in front of her.

"The native people of this area knew of this cave and of its magical properties. They believed it to be a passage from this world into the next. For several generations the ancients buried their people here. They believed the magic of the cave would ensure their journey into the afterlife. What they failed to understand is that this place is a world unto itself. It defies the boundaries of natural law. When the bodies of their ancestors were buried here, their souls became trapped in the crystals, consumed for all eternity by the Great Cave, their souls unable to move into the world of spirit.

"The second cavern we entered was smaller. The ceiling was right above us. The souls of the trapped spirits let out muffled cries. They do not bother my kind, but the woman's bright countenance darkened. A leaf-colored mist slowly surrounded our boat, followed by distinct voices calling out in agony. The woman spoke, asking me about the nature of this place. I gestured that this was the source of the magic she was seeking. She shook and held herself, as if afraid she would break apart.

"We ventured into the third cavern, where the walls opened up into a massive burial site filled with countless bones and gold offerings from the native peoples. Against the back wall, a row of skulls with their eyeless holes called out to us. The woman let out a shriek.

"The water beneath us glowed with the same color as the mist, and the crystals around the wall lit up, casting light into the far corners of the cave. I stifled a giggle at what I knew was coming next. My kin and I closed in on her. I dug my nails into her hands, trapping them to the edges of the boat while one of my comrades jumped onto her back and the other held down her hair, locking her to the center of the boat, preventing any attempt to escape. We may be small, but we are strong—stronger than humans give us credit for.

"I looked into her eyes and harnessed the magic around me to speak to her without words: *This is what you wanted; the source of our magic, the magic of the rainforest. It is bubbling beneath you. Can you feel it?*

"I took one of her hands and placed it on the surface of the glowing water. She let out a guttural scream and pulled back her arm, clutching the smoking remains of a blackened stump where her hand once resided. The Cave accepted her offering and we continued on.

"We journeyed past the graveyard of bones and to the final destination of our voyage. The hinges of reality were losing their grip on the woman. Her eyes grew wild and darted in every direction while she clutched her smoldering wrist.

"First, we felt the steady drumbeat as it vibrated up our bodies from beneath the water until we in turn, thrummed to the same rhythmic beat. Then we heard it, a sound so deafening it forced the woman to shake her head from side to side.

"The last cavern was the size of the previous three combined. In the center, hanging from a complex crystalline web, was an enormous black beating heart that moved and shifted with each rhythmic pulse. Its outer layer was slick with an oil-like substance, and veins ran along its exterior. As we got closer, the beating quickened, and we saw movement beneath its surface. Hands appeared, pushing from the inside of the rubbery shell, looking for a way out.

"The woman let out another scream. This time it was long and deep, reaching a primal part of herself.

"*This is the part of the rainforest that houses all that decays*, I explained again without words. *As death comes and the life force leaves, it is transmuted into energy for new life to exist. The energy of decay that cannot be reused, which is so far removed from life as to be unusable, is kept here to rot for all eternity. The magic that you seek takes its power from this beating heart.*

"We have taken many humans down to this cave over the years, but few survived long enough to witness the magnificence of the heart. This woman was special, she saw through our charms and survived the offering, and was now looking at the heart with a mixture of terror and awe. I sensed part of her was still holding onto the myth that somehow she could harness and control this power. We let go of our hold on her and positioned ourselves on the edges of the boat once more.

"A wet sucking sound echoed within the vast cavern as one of the heart's veins separated from its surface, followed by another, then another, until three long black veins wiggled like earthworms, searching for their quarry. The tip of one of the veins caressed the woman's face, leaving a black oily streak on her cheek while another slipped behind the nape of her neck. The remaining strand wrapped around her waist. The hold on her tightened as the heart beat in a rhythmic fervor, pumping and squeezing like an anaconda consuming its prey.

"The woman struggled to free herself, fearing—*knowing*—that she would no longer see anything outside of these cave walls. This only made the veins grip tighter, until one by one we heard her bones break, then her gasps for air. Her life force trickled out of her body. The veins became excited and shook as a predator does once it has conquered its kill. The veins drank up her soul through the tips until there was nothing left but an empty shell, then recoiled back to their place on the outside of the heart. The beating of the black heart slowed, and from within it we saw a new hand emerge, pushing up against the oily wall."

Ixikili widened her grin as she remembered this final scene in the cave. She stepped back into the outer ring of the circle as her colleagues applauded her tale with great enthusiasm.

"What a wonderful story, Ixikili, thank you." Noctis nodded in approval. The hourglass nearly emptied, Noctis turned and looked onto her fellow members of the dark. "Who's next?"

From a tree branch above flew an enormous creature with a wingspan that stretched as wide as the circle below. It stood nearly ten feet tall, and folded its massive, leathery wings behind it. Its red, piercing eyes glowed as it stepped into the light. Noctis turned the hourglass.

In a high-pitched voice that sounded forced and electronic, the being began, "Greetings, my fellow Night Members. I have been called many names over the centuries, the original people of the land called me Thunderbird, others Mothman. I am neither. I am not a being from their gods; I am neither a prophet nor a harbinger of doom. I am my own being, not beholden to any higher power or limited by anyone's beliefs. And that is the name of my tale: *I Am Not Who You Think I Am*."

***

"I, like many of you here, have roamed this planet for millennia. I do not remember my birth. I only remember coming into *being*. I do not believe that we are born like humans, we simply manifest into existence. Why, or by whom, has never been something that I questioned. I am here now, and that is all that matters. Humans spend too much time contemplating their existence and look at where it has gotten them. But I digress.

"My story took place last autumn, when the leaves started to fall and the nights grew long. I, like most of you here, am nocturnal, so I welcomed the return of the dark skies. During one of my nightly flights, I came upon a group of humans gathered around a campfire in the woods, much like us here tonight. There were four of them, three males and one female.

"They appeared young for their kind, and yet far past the age of innocence. I found a tree high enough that they would not be able to detect me, and yet close enough that I could hear them. The young woman spoke, 'No, you guys got it all wrong. That's not what the Mothman is. He came from the silos where they housed all that chemical waste crap leftover from the war. That's what my uncle said and he was there at Point Pleasant when the bridge collapsed.'

"'Sally, your uncle wouldn't know a grizzly bear from a snake. He's so far down a bottle half the time I don't know why you'd listen to him in the first place. Nah, Mothman came from the curse. Once the white man came and decimated the Shawnee, Chief Cornstalk cursed the people and the land for all eternity. That's when the Mothman came into being. And ever since, he's been roaming the area of West Virginia, keeping tabs on the white man, making sure we don't get too far out into the woods. 'Cuz I heard that's where he lives with his whole family; the Mothlady and their Mothbabies.' They all laughed at that last comment.

"Then another continued, 'Mothbabies? You're too much, Conrad. What you been smokin', and can I have some? No, you're both wrong. The Mothman is older than Point Pleasant and older than Chief Cornstalk's curse. There are drawings of it on the petroglyphs up in the Appalachian caves that go back hundreds, maybe thousands of years. No one knows who put them there or what they mean, and there are these spiral things all around it. If I had internet out here, I'd pull it up on my phone and show you.'

"The last one, a plump man with greasy hair, spoke next. 'Yeah, I've seen those too, Bernie, but I don't think it's of the Mothman. It might be some prehistoric bird like the Pterodactyl or something. Just because it's got wings doesn't mean it's automatically the Mothman.'

"'But those red eyes,' Bernie argued. 'The cave picture shows its red eyes. You mean to tell me that the Pterodactyl had red eyes? Plus the dinosaurs died out millions of years before the first human ever set foot on this planet. No, I stick with my original theory; it's the Mothman on those cave walls.'

"'Okay, Mr. Science Guy. So what if that's true? What if the Mothman is older than any of us thought? So what?' asked Sally.

"'So what?' Bernie was upset. 'That means we have no idea what it is or where it's from. We've had it wrong all these years. What if he's some alien dropped down from a spaceship and left here stranded with no way to get home?'

"'E.T. phone home!' shouted Conrad.

"'I'm serious!" cried Bernie. 'What if he's some scout sent from another alien race here to do reconnaissance on us, or worse, experiments?'

"'The dreaded anal probes!' They all laughed.

"'Look,' Bernie continued, 'all I'm saying is we don't know, and when we don't know, they have the upper hand. My vote is we hunt the beast down and kill it before it kills us. I mean, take all those cases of the Mothman popping up in the '60s. The creature kept pace with a car going a hundred miles per hour and left claw marks large enough to actually *dent* the hood. This thing isn't here passing out daisies and balloons, it literally tried to run those kids off the road. And let's take another look at the Silver Bridge collapse in '67. That bridge stood for nearly forty years, without fail, then this winged creature shows up all over town and *BAM*, the bridge collapsed. I mean, I don't believe in coincidences, do you guys?'

"'I see your point,' said Conrad. 'But was it here to warn of the bridge before it happened, or did Mothman actually cause the collapse? That's the question I struggle with.'

"'What kind of warning is it when you run alongside cars scaring the holy shit out of teenagers? That's not much of a warning if you ask me,' Sally added.

"'Yeah, I agree. I don't think it was here to warn. I actually think the thing caused the collapse,' the fat one uttered.

"'See what I mean? You guys get me. I think it was here to do us harm. I think it did cause the bridge to collapse—and you know what else? My dad and my cousin Jim think they saw it out past the Henderson Farm last month. And there have been more sightings up in Jackson, too. I mean, this thing may still be around here. And I'm not up for it killing more people. It needs to be stopped.' Bernie puffed up his chest then, as if to look bigger. The others were in agreement with him. I heard these versions of events countless times before. Humans are incredibly predictable. They like to blame others when something goes wrong. The truth is they did not build that bridge correctly, and with the winter ice and the heavy load of cars it simply gave out. I had nothing to do with it."

The creature paused and stared with its crimson eyes into his audience. "I do not feed in the traditional sense, for I do not have the physical need for food like some do. I feed off fear. I absorb fear into my being and that is what sustains me. I was there the night the bridge collapsed, feeding off the fear that was emanating from the disaster. It was a buffet that sustained me for decades afterward. Now sitting in my perch high above, hearing these humans tell their ridiculous version of events, I became … hungry.

"I slowly opened my wings, creating a breeze and a slight slapping sound until they looked up towards my direction. I focused my gaze on the one called Bernie. From my distance, all he could see were my eyes. I flew to another tree in the opposite direction, they turned to follow me, but their inferior sight could not penetrate the darkness. I flew closer, finding a perch no more than ten feet above them, and yet they were still unable to see me. But they sensed my presence.

"'What the hell was that?' asked one.

"'Dude, stop playing around, that's not funny,' said another.

"'I'm not doing anything.'

"'What was that over there? Did you guys see that?'

"'All I saw were red eyes, man. I'm fucking out of here.'

"'No wait, it's probably just an owl.'

"'Fuck you dude, that was no owl. That thing is huge; what if we drew out the Mothman talking like this?' asked Conrad.

"'You're all being ridiculous. I grew up in these woods, there's nothing out there to be afraid of. Whatever it is should be afraid of my .45,' Sally said as she patted the firearm on her hip.

"I'm sure most here will agree that when our prey is in a state of fear, their taste is so much more … delectable? No, rewarding. Yes, that's the word: rewarding.

"I flapped my wings again. When I start to feed, there is a sound that emanates from my being. It is a buzzing of sorts, like a swarm of bees that grows high-pitched, like cicadas.

"I was close enough for them to hear me buzzing above them. I swooped down to the ground, behind the one with a gun. I grabbed her from behind and flew back into the woods too fast for the others to see. I felt her terror and shook with delight. She was too afraid to reach for her gun. High up in the tree line, I embraced her, feeding off her until there was nothing left to take. Then I dropped her from a distance no human could survive.

"I was still hungry, so I returned to the campsite to find the three remaining humans scrambling towards their vehicle. Not one of them was brave enough to come after me when I took the woman; they were only concerned about themselves. How has this species survived so long?

"Before they reached their car, I landed hard on the roof, denting it with my weight, preventing them from opening up the doors. They scattered into the woods in opposite directions. And the hunt was on. The irony was not lost on me that a few minutes earlier they wanted to hunt me down and now, with me in their sights, what do they do? They run.

"The large one was the easiest to get, though a bit slippery. He barely made it twenty feet before I swooped down on him. I needed my talons to maintain my grip; he was so sweaty. As I consumed him, I tasted all the fears from his childhood; his being bullied in his teenage years, and his rejections by the opposite sex. It was delightful.

"Next, I tracked down the one called Conrad, who had been hiding in the marsh not far from the campsite. I saw him clearly trying to hide within the reeds. It was of no use; I flew down and grabbed him and consumed him mid-air, then dropped him back down into the reeds.

"Finally, I set my sights on Bernie, now deep in the woods. I tracked his body heat with my eyes. He was hiding in the base of a hollowed tree trunk. I landed directly in front of him and spread my wings. The scream he let out made the hackles on my spine shake. I was buzzing all over, feeding off his fear. I let him see me fully and spoke to him, 'I am not what you think I am.' I held him and squeezed him until he gave up his last drop. His hair turned white, and I detected that his eyes no longer housed a soul. He was a shell, still alive but with little or no brain function. Drool slipped from his mouth and ran down his chin. I rose then, back into the night, and have not had the need to feed since."

Applause erupted, some even stood to give a standing ovation as the creature known as the Mothman bowed and flew back onto his perch above the circle.

"Well now," said Noctis. "I think that made us all a little hungry, am I right?" She looked around and surveyed the crowd who nodded in agreement. "Thank you for that delectable story. Now, the moon is beginning to fall, we have time for just a few more. Who would like to go next?"

A dragging sound came from the left corner of the circle as something moved towards the firelight. The base of the creature was rotund and wet, with gray and brown spots like that of a walrus. The upper half was a radiant creature of unmatched beauty, a woman's countenance, with bare breasts and hair that hung in strands down her delicate shoulders, the color of glowing fire.

"Greetings to you all." The sound of her voice was like soft velvet as she drew her audience in. "My name is Salendra. I am from the great waters of the west. My sisters and I live on several islands hundreds of miles from the nearest continent. We have everything we need and want for nothing, save for one thing. My tale is titled, *The Face is Mine.*"

\*\*\*

"Our home is a paradise unto itself. We are the daughters of the great Poseidon, who abandoned this planet long ago. We are all that remain of his children, and there are only a few of us left. In the Old World, we outnumbered men. We were as plentiful as the fish, and our kind spanned across all oceans.

"Before modern day navigation, boats often got lost in our waters and storms pushed them into our home. Those were glorious times. We had our fun, took our fill, then left them to their watery graves. During the summer months, boats appear in the distance as they traverse the waters, but rarely do we interact with humans these days. So this past June when the waters were warm and the sun was high in the sky, my sisters and I were elated to see a boat not fifty meters from where we swam. The boat was small—too small to be navigating ocean waters, and we smelled only one occupant, a male.

"My sisters and I watched the boat meander without direction, having lost its rudder. We surrounded the vessel and waited for the man to emerge. We were giddy with delight. We had not seen a man this close in nearly a century. The anticipation warmed my insides.

"Loud screaming came from beneath the deck as a tan specimen emerged from the hull of the boat, a large metal tool in his hand and a grease stain on his forehead. He was beautiful to look upon. His lean physique glistened with sweat in the afternoon sun. He was naked, save for a blue patch of denim around his waist. My sisters and I flapped our tails with desire.

"My sister Jaquelina began singing her melodic tune. After all these years, her voice is still the most beautiful sound on Earth. We are all gifted with the ability to sing, a gift given to us by our father, but Jaquelina is the best among us. The notes she reaches can cause birds to fall out of the sky, and incapacitate all who come within a hundred leagues of it.

"The man stopped what he was doing and looked in our direction. We all ducked under the water, toying with him. Jaquelina sang again, then one by one the rest of us followed, adding our voices from every direction. One of us splashed up against the boat to make him investigate, and then another did the same on the opposite side. It was great fun. We did this until he was in a frothy state of agitation.

"I rose out of the water to face him, allowing him to see my face and the tops of my breasts. His agitation turned into lust, and I smelled his seed as it coursed through his cock. My sisters and I sang in unison; a pulsating tune with the power to entrance all who hear it.

The man walked, as if drugged, to the end of the boat and straight into the water without hesitation. We were on him then, all four of us grabbed a part of him. He did not struggle; instead, he gave into his carnal desires and let us consume him. The face—his face was mine. Peering into his eyes, I knew he wanted me with every ounce of his being. That look continues to invade my dreams to this day. He was enraptured as my sisters pulled off a limb and his blood mixed with the blue of the sea. I kissed him before he lost consciousness, locking him in my embrace. Holding his head in my hands, I drove my tongue deeper into his skull, feeling his ecstasy, tasting his essence. My nails dug into the back of his skull and once I found purchase, I pulled his scalp towards me, as if peeling a grapefruit. I released him from my kiss and saw his sandy hair float in the water like wings flapping in the sky. The back of his head was no longer attached to his skull, and I pulled harder towards me. A cloud of red arose behind him.

I continued to pull until I came to his cheeks, his chin, his nose, and finally, those deep blue eyes—I gave one final yank, and he was free. His face was in my hands. I kicked the rest of his body away from me, as I had no further use for it. My sisters consumed the remains. The prize I wanted was in my hands, his face. I gazed into the bloody visage with empty holes where the eyes used to be, and kissed it once more, before devouring it whole. The face ... the face is the tastiest bit."

Salendra looked off into the night sky as she stroked her breasts; lost in the memory of her most recent conquest. She caught herself and came back to the present, looking at the eyes around the campfire, and she blew a kiss to the crowd.

Whistles, hisses and cheers, mixed with applause, erupted in the night sky as the audience gave their enthusiastic approval of Salendra's story.

"Well now, my dear." Noctis fanned herself. "That was an arousing tale indeed. Maybe we can work together to bring more stranded sailors to your shores. Wouldn't that be nice?" More raucous applause from the crowd.

A being stepped into the light, and as he did, all within the crowd bowed in reverence to the one they all called Master.

Noctis gave a low bow. "Master, you grace us with your presence. You are very welcome. How may we serve you?"

"Arise. For tonight, I am not here to seek anything from you." The being was radiant perfection, with a voice that penetrated the core of each creature. His golden countenance glowed brighter than the fire which had now begun to die down. He wore a black suit, with a matching black tie made of the finest silk. His hair was of the same golden shade as his aura, and his wings, the color of crow feathers, were folded back behind him.

"I am simply here to tell my tale, one I shall call *The Hubris of Man.*" He turned his attention to Noctis. "You may start the hourglass."

Noctis obediently flipped the timer and bowed once more.

***

"Many of you here know that I leave my home rarely these days. I prefer instead to have my servants venture out to execute my will." He nodded towards Clarion, who fell prostrate upon the ground. "But there are occasions when the work can only be done by Yours Truly. And I have to get *my hands dirty*, as the saying goes. This was one of those times.

"I have endured many falsities since the dawn of civilization. I am resigned to my role as the opposite of the Light, for I provide balance and order through the chaos that I bring. I understand my role and I do it well. I, however, do not force or make humans bend to my will; I simply show them who they really are, revealing the carnal nature that lies beneath their cultured façade.

"There are some humans who I interact with more than others, again saving the bulk of the work for my competent foot soldiers. Take Rachel, for instance. Her heart is as dark as my most trusted generals. I had to meet her for myself and perhaps groom her to join my ranks at a later date. She was an exception, as I rarely get involved in individual cases. I instead choose to devote my energy towards grander designs: war, politics, global warming, mass shootings and the like. So it was odd when a fair few in my employ came to me with a task they were unable to perform.

"I was in my chambers, ruminating about starting a war in Angola, when a handful of my sergeants requested an audience. I put down my work and granted them permission to speak. They reported that several of my demon infantry had gone missing. They failed to report back to their stations and were not detectable on this plane or the earth plane. Some had been missing for nearly a year.

"I take pride in running an orderly operation. Our function of instilling chaos demands a level of discipline to execute. All those within my purview are required to check in with their superior officer when out in the field. They provide progress reports and are mentored by senior staff to make sure the work is completed to my satisfaction. Failure to do so would be unwise, for I do take great pride in the punishments I create. There is a special place in Hell reserved for those who disobey *my* orders. Few, if any, ever do.

"I was alarmed they did not bring this to my attention sooner. When asked, they cowered in fear of my disapproval. The missing all went after the same target; a male who was an advocate for the Great Opposing One. Each time a soldier was sent out, they would disappear, unable to be tracked by our systems. More alarming, one of my most trusted Lieutenants, Beelzebub, went looking for the missing and ended up disappearing as well.

"I was troubled indeed, for there had not been such a disturbance in hell since the Adversary's Son came into our realm. I asked for the full report on this human while I prepared for my earth-bound trip.

"The dimension of hell, as most of you here can attest, is quite different from that of Earth. I had not stepped onto this plane for several centuries, so it took a bit of time adjusting to the heaviness of its gravity. In my realm I am used to being able to take flight without a thought, and coming here requires a … recalibration of sorts. When I emerged from our dimension into the next, I ended up falling—unable to take flight, as my wings became heavier in this atmosphere. Unlike my foot soldiers who can be in their ethereal form when on this plane, this time I chose to materialize my whole being so as to be fully prepared for whatever lay ahead.

"I landed hard on the Earth's surface. As I stood, I was struck by the abundance of light. A pair of darkened lenses helped my vision adjust. I scoured my surroundings and felt a pull in one direction. It was something I had not felt before, which is unusual for someone who has been in existence since the dawn of time. This pull—from the center of my being, felt like a tug from a rope. I sensed a conjuring of sorts; someone was summoning the dark, as if a vacuum were drawing the energy in. After concealing my wings, I adopted this human countenance which you see before you, and journeyed towards the source.

"Outstretched in front of me, stood an ornate building, one that filled an entire street and stretched high into the clouds. The spires atop reminded me of the Silver City, where I originated. The structure was white with windows of various colors, and a massive entrance that rivaled the Great Gates of Hell. This was the source of the disturbance, a church devoted to the Opposing One.

"The heat outside was sweltering; it reminded me of home except for the heavy moisture in the air. The alarming cry of cicadas pierced my senses, giving a warning of what was to come. I arrived on the day dedicated to the worship of the Other; where humans gather in their praise for a God that does not even know they exist.

"There was a score of vehicles out front, indicating the number inside to be vast. I took my time and walked around the perimeter, assessing the energy shifts within. There was powerful sorcery here, the likes not seen since dragons roamed the skies. The pull strengthened as I ventured towards the back of the building. Raucous music and singing emanated from inside the white stucco walls. There was also a familiar scent, the slight aroma of brimstone. My wards had been there. Locks on a set of tinted glass doors, fell upon the ground with a wave of my hand, and I ventured within.

"The smell of coffee was brewing to my right and the odor of urine to my left. A series of rooms emerged, each with a specific purpose. I discovered a great hall, which was empty save for a series of chairs stacked on top of each other, and a counter towards the back with an array of sweet foods and Styrofoam cups. Beyond this was a small cooking area which housed a variety of tools and equipment. In each room there were black stains, as if scorched by fire in every corner. But these discolorations were not seen with the physical eye, they were more of a psychic impression, a cloud clinging to each corner. The tar-like imprints were not visible at first, but the longer I stayed in each space the more discernible the darkness became.

"As I travelled down another hall, I sensed the innocent being held in a room to my left. Peering into a window at the door, several children were playing with toys in a brightly colored room. The adult woman did not notice me but a few of the children did. As they looked in my direction, I removed my lenses to reveal flames where human eyes should be. One by one they began to wail, until the entire room was a sea of screams. I continued on.

"I came upon a narrow staircase with rips and stains in the carpet that stood out from the rest of the pristine interior. Thick black stains dripped down the walls like melted wax. I was starting to admire the illusion. The power of this energy was becoming tangible.

"As I approached the top of the stairs, the heaviness of the Earth's gravity became more forceful. My wings felt like ship anchors weighing down my back. It took effort for me to lift my head to see what was before me. The room was painted a dull beige, stark save for a circle of empty chairs in the center of the room. As I approached the circle, the pull and heaviness intensified. There was a shimmering of light in the center, from which a dark mass emerged. In an instant I knew what appeared before me, and I was impressed.

"These humans learned how to harness the energy of space. They conjured up a black hole within their plane. And what was equally remarkable was their ability to *control* the void, for I sensed only darkness within it, as if it was able to distinguish light from dark. The smell of my fallen soldiers was prominent in this room; they must have been trapped in this interdimensional prison.

"The singing below me suddenly ceased. Within a few moments chatter erupted in the kitchen beneath my feet, followed by the clanking of plates. I stood motionless, taking in my surroundings and planning my next move. After a time, the cars outside started, their engines fading as they drove off into the distance. The noise beneath me died down as the building emptied. A handful of voices reached the foot of the stairs. It took great effort for me to move, but I managed. A space behind the doorway provided me with cover, hiding me in the shadows.

"Five humans, of no distinct consequence, entered the room. Each took a seat around the black hole. I did not sense any power emanating from them, except one. I recognized him immediately from the case file. Every aspect of him was round. He had a round head, round limbs, round torso—even his fingers were rounded. There was not a straight line or edge or point anywhere in his makeup. He was circular; there was nothing hard about him. And he had a distinct smell, coffee mixed with cologne and sweat and something else I could not decipher, a hint of wetness, perhaps.

"As I continued to observe, one of the females began to speak. 'Pastor John, that was a powerful sermon today. I really felt the Holy Spirit speaking through you.'

"'Yes,' said another, 'and that part about Noah and his Ark being a metaphor for us to carry our own with us into salvation touched me deep in my core.' Then the object of my quest spoke. 'You are both too kind. I was moved by the Lord today and am just the messenger for his good news. It struck a chord because it is the truth.' He paused, closed his eyes, and said, 'Now, let us begin.'

"They proceeded to hold hands with each other in the circle and closed their eyes. Their bodies swayed rhythmically to the beat of a silent drum. The main one spoke again in a deeper voice then before, *'Vocamus in potentia vacui. Vocamus in potentia vacui. Vocamus in potentia vacui.'* The shimmering in the circle became more pronounced, and a doorway formed.

"The atmosphere in the room changed and I dug my nails deep into the wooden frame of the wall to keep myself from getting pulled in. As the hole widened, I heard the screams of my foot soldiers emanating from within. I was mystified at how these humans were able to conjure this.

"I listened further.

"*We call forth the dimension of the Whole, the Almighty, God the Father, God the Son, and God the Holy Spirit. All those who are of light shall remain in this realm, all those of the dark shall be fed into the void.*'

"They chanted in unison, '*All those of the dark shall be fed into the void, all light shall remain in this realm, all those of the dark shall be fed into the void, all light shall remain in this realm.*'

"A fury within me arose that I have not felt since I first fell. These humans, these meaningless nothings, were trying to alter the very nature of all that is. Every one of you here plays an important role in the balance of light and dark. We cannot have light without dark and we cannot have dark without light. That is the nature of the Grand Design that we are all a part of. We are no less important than the light for without us, *the light would not know itself.*

"I stood from the shadow and stepped before them. By now the black hole was spinning, causing the pressure in the room to drop. There was a deafening sound, and the force of a hurricane wind filled the entire building, causing it to shake down to its foundation. Objects beneath the floor began to move. Plates and chairs crashed beneath me, and doors throughout the building slammed shut.

"The only one to notice me was Pastor John. His eyes fixated upon me. I stepped closer and yelled, '*ENOUGH!*' They awoke from their trance and stared at me; the wind died down. The hole in the center continued to flicker. The closer I got, the more effort it took to prevent being sucked in.

"I continued, 'What you have done is a sin against your God, as it is a sin against nature. Who do you think you are to meddle with the laws of the universe, to bend them to your will? What hubris you have.'

"The round pastor spoke. 'So, you came, finally, you are here.

We have been waiting for your arrival, O Great One. We seek to bargain with you.' He stood now, leaving the circle and stepped closer to me. I understood the smell that eluded me earlier: the aroma of desire.

"He continued, 'All of us here are the top scientists in our fields. Collectively, we are at the forefront of mathematics, astrophysics and quantum physics, and unlocked the formula to the Einstein-Rosen Bridge which you see here before you. We created a vacuum in space, small enough to control with the boundaries we put upon it and yet strong enough to contain that which you see before you. We did this, all of this, to draw you here. We knew your demons would not be able to resist tempting the pastor of a megachurch. So we built one, and I became one. We knew that the larger the church became, the greater the prize for one of your employ. So we grew. All the while we were working on a particle accelerator, housed in the basement of this building, to create what you see here before you.'

"I was at a loss for words, which is a rarity for me. He explained further. 'If we could contain your demons and prevent them from returning to hell, we were sure it would draw you out, to come looking for them. And our theory was correct because here you are before us, Lucifer Morningstar, The Fallen One.'

"I was tempted to end them then, but first needed to free those trapped.

"'Clever,' I replied while calculating my next move, 'but short-sighted. I do not bend to anyone's will, let alone that of a group of humans. I serve my function as dictated by the Grand Design, and that is my only obligation.'

'But we need you, Lucifer, we need to understand—how can we find God? We have calculated the mathematical beginning of creation and discovered a unique frequency which we believe to be the Creator's energy. But we haven't been able to get close to the source, it still eludes us. You alone can help us find Him. Please tell us, how can we locate Him? And in exchange, we will gladly return your demons to you.'

"'And what would you do with God once you found Him?' I toyed with them.

"The pastor looked at his colleagues. 'We would ask why it is that we exist and what He truly intends for us, His creation.' The vacuum in the circle began to quiver.

"'Your ability to create this portal is impressive. What do you think you can do, create another and trap God within it?' I knew exactly what their intentions were, the same intention of the first man who walked upon this Earth.

"They looked at each other, not sure how to answer, so I continued, 'You cannot fool the Creator of Lies, for I invented the very nature of it. That is part of *my* creation. No. Your real intention is as clear to me as your feeble attempt to harness power you cannot dream of comprehending. There is a reason why your science has not been able to unlock certain doors. There are things you are not meant to know. You are incapable of accessing certain knowledge, because it would destroy you. Your very existence would cease to exist. Do you really think there is a *God* that you can converse with? Are you that naïve? There is no such thing. There are only those of us stationed to create order and chaos. That is all that exists. Nothing more.'

"The wholeness of my function came into form. My power grew as my wings expanded. Closer to the void, I sensed a vulnerability within its construction.

"I continued. 'No, you do not wish to speak to God, you want to become God. You want to harness that creative energy for yourselves. I admire your desire, but not your stupidity.' I walked around them and gazed into each of their eyes as they looked upon me. 'I grow tired of this. Enough.' Before they could protest, I joined them together into a singular mass. Each of their bodies merged into another, forming a gelatinous sludge. Torso against torso as limbs pressed together and their shoulders and heads merged. The sound of their screams as their bones were breaking towered over the sound of the void. Their skeletal structure became malleable, allowing for further cohesion until all was one.

Their cumulative fat muffled their screams. Their souls remained trapped, preventing escape and allowing their consciousness to remain fully aware of their pain and what was to come next. My hand waved the collective mass to the far corner of the room. I approached the void.

"I rolled up my sleeve and placed one arm into the portal. I dug the other into the floorboards for anchorage. My arm started to disintegrate, I had to act quickly. I called forth those trapped within, feeling them grab hold of my hand until one by one they formed a chain on the other side. I pulled, using all of my power, and eventually each one birthed through the portal—squeezing and gasping through a hole too small for their size. As the last one fell to the floor, I drew a doorway to Hell, which opened and swallowed them back into the abyss.

"Seeing the usefulness of this black hole, I created a seal around it and sent it to my chambers along with the particle accelerator in the basement. So now all that remained was the matter of the human mass in the corner.

"The giant pile of flesh stared up at me. The mass formed a singular consciousness, their eyes all blinked in unison. A mouth stuck out of a stomach, an ear attached to a kneecap, an eye peered out of an armpit. All was fluid and in constant motion as their bits swam across a sea of skin. A faint grunt emanated from the heap. Never again would they be able to utter a word.

"'Your hubris and your power lust were your own undoing. This fate you suffer now is of your own making. The void that you created had one critical flaw. It only captured those in their incorporeal states. I, as you can see—well, maybe you can no longer see—am in my true form. I stand before you in all of my presence: my physical, ethereal and astral bodies are here, now, in this one form. That is why I was able to reach into the portal without being sucked into it myself.

"'Oh, and by the way, the Creator Energy that you craved to meet, in order to harness and steal the power for yourself? Well,' I turned away from them and walked a few feet towards the door, 'you accomplished at least *part* of your task. It was a pleasure to meet you.' And with that I took my leave and returned to my home."

All eyes were fixed upon the storyteller.

After an uncomfortable silence, Noctis began to clap, and was quickly followed by raucous applause as accolades were showered upon the one they called Master. He took a deep bow and raised a glass to the group. In an instant, all members were holding a glass with a red bubbly liquid.

"To the Dark!" he shouted, and was echoed with "To the Dark!" from the crowd who lapped up the contents of their glasses.

"But Master," a tiny doll with reddish blonde hair and a missing eye stepped into the light, "what happened to the people who were in that blob?"

"Oh, them?" Satan answered coyly. "Well, I would not come to a gathering of my servants without bringing some sort of gift. What kind of master would I be if I did not show my appreciation from time to time? Bring it out."

Two red-faced demons with the bodies of toddlers came forward, pulling a series of chains attached to a fleshy ball of meat. Its eyes blinked in unison, mouths opening and closing like fish out of water.

"Now Noctis, my beautiful seductress, I would not wish to interfere with your proceedings here tonight. But may I propose that all who are gathered here partake in the gift I have provided?"

"Master," replied Noctis, "it would be our great honor to accept the gift you bestow upon us. You humble us with your presence and your generosity. And as the night is coming to a close, it is time to announce our winners."

Brother Leeds stepped forward immediately and shouted, "I propose that all prizes be awarded to the Dark Master for his tale, *The Hubris of Man.*"

"I second the proposal!" said a growl in the crowd.

"I third!" said another followed by a cry of 'Ayes'.

Noctis looked pleased. "Well then, we have a proposal to offer all three prizes to our Lord and Master. Any objections?"

A collective 'Nay' cut through the night air.

"Very well then. This year's third, second and Grand Prize winner of our storytelling contest goes to Satan, Lucifer Morningstar. May we continue to serve you our Lord, and be forever blessed by your darkness. Now, let's eat!"

# ABOUT THE AUTHOR

Francesca Maria writes dark fiction surrounded by cats near the Pacific Ocean. She is the creator of the *Black Cat Chronicles* comic book series and her short stories and essays can be found in various publications including: *Shallow Waters Special Halloween Edition*, *Death's Garden Revisited*, and on Crystal Lake's Patreon page. You can find her at francescamaria.com and on Twitter @Writer_of_Weird.

# ACKNOWLEDGEMENTS

This book would not be possible without a slew of people that helped me along the way. First off to my beta readers: Teresa Soito, L.S. Johnson, Rhokis Bane, and Mark Causey, I can't thank you enough for your thorough and thoughtful feedback. You helped make my collection clear and strong. To my editors, Karen Runge, Elle Turpitt and Stephanie Ellis for your keen eyes and your ability to help me avoid rookie mistakes, thank you. To the Bay Area HWA chapter members: Ben Monroe, Loren Rhoads, Sumiko Saulson, L.S. Johnson, Luke Neher, Elana Gomel and so many more, thank you for your encouragement and expertise. To my HWA mentor Christi Nogle, I have no words sufficient enough to express my gratitude for your wisdom and practical advice as I navigated this journey, thank you. And to the fine folks at Brigid's Gate Press: Steve and Heather, thank you for taking a chance on *They Hide*. You made a lifelong dream come true.

And last but definitely not least, to my biggest cheerleader and steadfast partner for over twenty-five years, my husband, Causey. Thank you for putting up with my creepy tendencies and for your continued willingness to read my horrific tales. I love you. Thank you.

# MORE FROM BRIGIDS GATE PRESS

A family's relocation looked like a chance to relax and regroup—but as they settle into their new home, teenage Kimmie Barnes' special senses make her the target of something primordial, evil, and utterly malign.

*Darkness…*

Golden Oaks, California is a sleepy town on the shores of Oro Lake, and the residents have no idea what horrors lurk below the glittering waters.

*Beneath the waves…*

One by one, as people begin to disappear, the once quiet town is soon in the grips of a waking nightmare.

An unimaginable horror consuming everything before it.

*Hungry…*

All while echoes of an ancient evil spread out like malignant spider webs, like dead hands reaching, grasping …

***SEETHING…***

A vengeful owl haunts the man who poached her. A desperate entrepreneur holds a ghost hostage for profit. An addict finds hope and terror in an imprisoned angel. A father and son search their dying world for something to eat other than human flesh. Eric Raglin, author of *Nightmare Yearnings*, returns with his second collection of horror and weird fiction. Strange, terrifying, and tender, these eighteen stories explore what happens when extinction comes for us all.

**In an Old West overrun by monsters, a stoic gunslinger must embark on a dangerous quest to save her friends and stop a supernatural war.**

Sharpshooter Melinda West, 29, has encountered more than her share of supernatural creatures after a monster infection killed her mother. Now, Melinda and her charismatic partner, Lance, offer their exterminating services to desperate towns, fighting everything from giant flying scorpions to psychic bugs. But when they accidentally release a demon, they must track a dangerous outlaw across treacherous lands and battle a menagerie of creatures— all before an army of soul-devouring monsters descend on Earth.

**The Witcher meets Bonnie and Clyde in a re-imagined Old West full of diverse characters, desolate landscapes, and fast-paced adventure.**

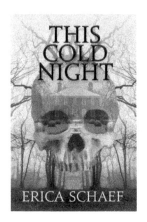

Following the death of a loved one, Rachelle Collins visits Ferguson Estate, an expansive country mansion which holds many fond memories, and one sinister secret, within its walls. Throughout the course of a single, terrifying night, Rachelle must confront horrors, both psychological and tangible, to prove just how far she is willing to go to keep her family together.

Visit our website at: www.brigidsgatepress.com

# CONTENT WARNINGS

**The Wysterfield Murders:** non-explicit rape, child death, religion, murder, misogyny, gore

**Shane O'Reilly:** murder, gore

**My Brother Andy:** murder, demons, child death

**The Perfect Partner:** sexually explicit scenes

**The Circus:** none

**The Legend of the Chupacabra:** none

**A Game of Ghost:** death, suicide

**Jean-Pierre de Rochet:** none

**Imhotep:** none

**Zombies Are Real:** animal death, death

**Wendigo:** death, gore

**Spreckles:** child abuse, child death, murder, death, gore

**The Gathering:** death, murder, gore, child abuse, child death, pedophilia, demons

Printed in the USA
CPSIA information can be obtained
at www.ICGtesting.com
LVHW091639061023
760258LV00001B/48